KAPOWIE!

PINX VIDEO MYSTERIES

MARSHALL THORNTON

Published by Kenmore Books

Edited by Joan Martinelli

Cover design by Marshall Thornton

Images by 123rf stock, captainvector

ISBN:

First Edition

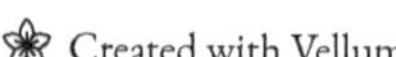 Created with Vellum

ACKNOWLEDGMENTS

A big thank you to: Joan Martinelli, Nathan Bay, Tina Greene Bevington, Shanee Edwards, Danielle Wolff, Chris Carter, and Ben Thompson.

CALL SHEET

FINN HENDERSON – The star of megahits like *Crushed for Glory*, *Patriot's Choice* and *Save Her*, Finn began his career with *Kapowie!* And now he's back to tell us all about his time on the show! Famous for his blue eyes and chiseled jaw, he has won hearts in the romantic comedies *Sleeping With Bees* and *Heartfelt*. After years of wrestling with personal demons, Finn is making his comeback in the upcoming thriller *Running Toward Justice*. Perhaps he'll share a bit about that.

AMBER BRIGHT – CEO of Bright Management, Ms. Bright dedicates herself to handling Finn Henderson's career. Always presenting herself crisply and professionally, she navigates the pressures of Finn's publicity, career choices, daily meetings, rehearsals, fittings and everything else that makes a major film star's life run smoothly.

KATHLEEN TRUE – After her time as the "It" girl of *Kapowie!*, Kathleen married televangelist Winthrop True and began appearing on his show *True Faith*. Quickly, she became the darling of Believe Television Network. Famous for her silvery hair and expressive makeup, Kathleen prides herself on personally bringing thousands of souls to the Lord.

HESTON TRUE – Teenaged son of Kathleen and Winthrop True, this stunning young man is poised to choose whether to follow in the footsteps of his father *or* his mother. Stay tuned for a jaw-dropping announcement on that front.

WES LANGE – A beloved member of the *Kapowie!* cast, during his time on the show he caused many female friendships to fracture as girls all over the country argued over who was sexier: Finn or Wes? The mysterious Mr. Lange has dropped out of the public eye, but for our show, he just might make an appearance. Wait and see.

GRACE HORLOCK – If you live in Los Angeles, you know our Grace. She's *the* premiere luxury real estate agent and her gorgeous face adorns countless bus benches and billboards. Elegant and timeless, Grace would have gone far had she remained an actress. Well, she'll just have to console herself with piles of money!

RICKY BELLOWS – His is the classic story. During his time on the show Ricky was the original nerd, a ninety-nine-pound weakling. But through grit and determination, he's turned himself into a muscle-bound Adonis. *And* he's now an entrepreneur, owning three gymnasiums.

DR. MEG RODGERS – Well, not a medical doctor. Something to do with plants. Like many single women in their thirties, Meg teaches. Science. Still carrying a bit of baby fat, she lives with her two cats and practices recipes with which to snare herself a husband.

KEELY FAIRING – Our girl from the inner city, Keely was always a bright and energetic presence on the show, with her lovely singing voice and innate ability to dance. Though she's left show business and returned to her roots owning a florist shop in Leimert Park, we still have to wonder if she misses the glitz and glamour of being a TV star.

MARC JANES – Little Marc was our youngest cast member and the funniest. Now an accountant—yes, we had to ask if he was joking—we suspect Marc is the funniest accountant on the West Coast.

DONALD AND WENDY BARCLAY – Our producers. Donald and Wendy produced both of the original seasons of *Kapowie!* They are so excited to be back in show business! Taking a break from their chain of Juicy Juice stores, the Barclays are thrilled to be flexing their creative muscles once again. Rumor has it good things are on the horizon for them.

ED BLINSKI – Our intrepid grip and jack-of-all-trades, Ed works during the week at a Juicy Juice in North Hollywood.

LOUIS DOISER – Craft services. We've been promised some delightful yummies.

NOAH VALENTINE – Helper number one.

ELDRIDGE HALL – Helper number two.

ONE

The whole thing began, as things often do with us, on a Thursday night. It was mid-June, and we were sitting outside in the courtyard of our small, L-shaped apartment building in Silver Lake. The giant birds of paradise were in full flower and there was a night-blooming jasmine doing its thing nearby. It was around eight, and the setting sun had driven the temperature down under seventy. Fortunately, I was wearing a blue jean shirt over a black tee, like a jacket.

Marc and Louis were both wearing the peeling sunburns they'd gotten the previous Sunday at Pride. I didn't go. Instead, I'd worked at Pinx Video all by myself so my staff could go. Trust me, that was not as generous as it sounds. Spending the afternoon with a couple hundred thousand gay people is an amazing experience—the first couple of times. Eventually, it becomes an exercise in getting pushed around, stepped on, gawked at, losing your friends, drinking too much beer, and getting a scorching sunburn. I'll probably go next year.

The details on the where-are-they-now episode of *Kapowie!* had fallen into place and would be shooting in two days. Marc had convinced the producers to hire Louis to do craft services, mainly so we could all be there, but also... the money. They were still stashing away every penny they could get their hands on to buy a house after one had fallen through in January. Or rather, nearly fallen down and then fallen through. Louis needed two helpers—well, knowing Louis he probably didn't, but he'd insisted on two—so now *he* had to come up with them.

"Absolutely not," Leon said stridently. "I'm a dom not a sub."

"I'm not asking you to be submissive," Louis said. "I'm asking you to be a cater waiter for one night."

"Honestly, I don't see the difference. I will not submit."

I nearly choked on the white lasagna I was eating. Which would have been a shame since it was delicious. How could Leon refuse to go? *I* was going to refuse to go. Well, not refuse exactly. More like politely decline. But I couldn't do that if Leon refused. I couldn't leave Louis completely in the lurch. Could I?

"Won't you do it for me, Leon?" Marc asked, dramatically batting his eyelashes.

"Darling, you know I'd kill for you. I just won't cater. Or for that matter do any other sort of menial labor."

"In other words, you wouldn't lift a finger for me."

"I'm glad we understand each other," Leon said before sipping his glass of white wine.

To Louis, Marc said, "I thought for sure he'd say yes once he found out Finn Henderson would be there."

In case your name is Gilligan and you've been living on a deserted island, Finn Henderson is a big movie star—well, he was until a nasty heroin addiction and multiple arrests sidelined him. He'd been at Betty Ford most of '92 and into '93, and had just shot a new movie that was already getting a lot of buzz. He was on the brink of a comeback. The *Kapowie!* producers were thrilled when he agreed to revisit the show that had given him his start.

"I'd love to get up close and personal with Finn Henderson," Leon said. "But trust me. 'Would you like a Perrier?' is not the conversation I'd like to have with him."

Marc rolled his eyes.

"Well, at least we can count on Noah," Louis said.

That was my opportunity to speak up and explain all the reasons I couldn't do it. I was too busy with Pinx—which was not true. I had enough employees, and as nearly as I could tell the shoot wasn't taking place during business hours. My health was not good—except it was. I was feeling better than I'd felt in a long time. And, and... But those were the only two excuses I could come up with. Still, I should at least try to get out of it.

"The thing is—"

"I was wondering," Louis said to me. "Can you help me find someone? To replace our useless friend over here."

"What? Me? Couldn't you call a catering company? And I don't know that Leon is useless. I mean, not completely."

"Thank you. Such glowing praise."

"You have employees," Louis said. "Could we ask one of them?"

This was not going well. I really should hold my ground and say no. Particularly since now it wouldn't just be me helping them out, we'd be involving one of my employees. With a deeply frustrated sigh, I said, "Well, Mikey's a bad idea. He'll try to run everything. And Carl and Denny only work as a team."

"What about the new guys?" Marc asked.

"Ryan is absolutely out of the question," I said, immediately. "The porno thing."

"Oh, yeah," Louis said. "There's that."

I liked Ryan. A lot. He was good to have around the store. He just liked the porn section a little too much, and since one of Marc's castmates was Ricky Bellows, well... And in case you don't remember *him*, he's the one whose ex-girlfriend sold their sex tape to Verve Video and everyone who saw it was very *impressed* by Ricky. Of course, he threatened to sue but eventually dropped it. That was probably a ruse to get even more publicity. Long story short, the gym he owns in Reseda is now a chain.

The sex tape angle made it a bad idea to let Ryan anywhere

near him. He might ask for an autograph with black marker—on his butt.

"What about Eldridge?" Louis suggested.

"Yeah, he'll do it," Marc said. "He has such a crush on you."

"Oh, he does not. And how would you know?"

"Duh, we rent videos from you. We've seen the way he looks at you."

Everyone at the table raised an eyebrow at me. Nightmare. Complete nightmare. Now I was going to spend eight hours doing something I didn't want to do with someone I didn't want to spend time with. Well, I didn't *not* want to spend time with him. And I did spend time with him at the store. Well, some. Admittedly, I spent a lot of time in my office. Anyway, the whole thing was—complicated.

"He is awfully cute," Louis said.

"Stop trying to push us together," I said. "He's too young for me. Okay?"

"Nine years," Marc said. "It's the perfect age gap. Louis is ten years older than I am."

That didn't leave me a lot of room to complain without being rude. Anyway, I'd always been interested in guys who were *older* than I am. And then there was the fact that Eldridge worked for me, which would be awkward if it didn't work out. Which it wouldn't because, well, I'm me.

Since Jeffers died, I'd been interested in three guys, two of whom are now dead. And the third is, well, a mess. And not in a good way. All of which left me in the precarious position of not wanting to date people I actually liked.

"I'm not going to date him. But I will ask if he'd like to pick up a little extra money. If I have to."

"You have to," Louis said.

Eldridge was a student at UCLA, so it was likely he could use some extra cash. And I couldn't say no to helping out a college kid, could I? Well, I did want to say no to the whole thing, but clearly that wasn't happening.

"You said Saturday. What time—"

Leon interrupted by asking, "Is *Kathleen* going to be there?" He gave the former child star-turned-televangelist's name the annoying spin it deserved.

"Everyone's going to be there except Wes Lange," Marc said. "Apparently, no one can find him."

"You know, I always thought he was much sexier than Finn Henderson," Louis said. "All that blond hair."

"Most people did," Marc said. "In person. Something about him didn't translate on camera."

"Anyway, I was asking about the time to—"

"Getting back to *Kathleen*," Leon said. "You are going to slip a laxative into her food, aren't you? The idea of her shitting her panties is just too delicious."

Kathleen True had been the sexpot on *Kapowie!*, always dressing in the workout gear of the late seventies, foreshadowing the fitness craze of the eighties. During the show she was eighteen and nineteen, and, to the horror of the network executives, was 'connected' to several older movie stars. But mostly she was Finn Henderson's girlfriend.

After the show ended they broke up and she'd gone on to marry Winthrop True, the televangelist with the church next to the 5 freeway down in Orange County. She had a regular segment on her husband's show, *True Faith*, and was prone to crying jags in which she asked God to smite the gays. Or so I've heard. It's the last thing in the world I'd actually watch.

"Time? What time is all this happening?"

"I always find it interesting that no matter how many times she asks we never get smote," Leon said.

Louis said, "I don't think she'd see it that way."

"What do you mean?"

"Uh, AIDS?!"

"Yeah, but that's..." Leon got an angry look on his face. "So, when an eight-year-old gets cancer, that's God smiting a child?"

"No, that's God loving your child so much he wanted him in heaven."

"So it never occurs to anyone that maybe God wants some gays to liven things up? I mean, the heaven people like Kathleen are planning sounds dreadfully dull. I can't image a God who doesn't love a fabulous party."

As forcefully as possible, I said, "I've been trying to ask—"

"What darling?" Leon said. "Spit it out."

"What *time* is all this happening?!" I took a breath, then calmly added, "I'll need to tell Eldridge."

"We need to gather at the south gate of Bennett Day Studios in Culver City at ten forty-five," Louis said. "The producers are being very weird about it. They keep strongly repeating the instructions."

"Ten-forty-five Saturday morning, got it."

"No, no, no. Ten-forty-five Saturday *night*."

"Night? Wait, you mean we're working all night? Why are we doing that?"

Like I said, this was a nightmare. One with sequels.

"Well obviously it's cheaper," Marc said. "I have no idea how small the budget is, but I'm sure it's minuscule. Even if it weren't, the producers are notoriously cheap. I'm only getting scale plus ten."

"So it's the same producers?"

"Donald and Wendy Barclay. I don't think they ever worked again after *Kapowie!* I've had three phone calls with them and every time they mention how great it is to be back in the biz. Well, Donald says that; Wendy doesn't seem as excited."

"So how much am I getting?"

"Fifteen an hour."

That wasn't horrible. And Eldridge would be happy. It was more than the nine dollars an hour I was paying him, and that was more than double minimum wage.

Lewis brought out dessert. A vanilla walnut parfait that was amazingly good. When he sat back down again, he asked, "Have you been following the O.J. thing?"

"A little," I admitted.

"A little?" Leon said. "I'm glued to it!"

Then Marc said, "Apparently his ex-wife's therapist is in all sorts of trouble for talking about things she said in therapy. Things about O.J. beating her and threatening her."

"They found a bloody glove at his house," Louis said, simply.

"Do you think they're going to arrest him?" Marc asked.

"I wouldn't be surprised."

The guys talked a bit more about the things they'd heard on TV. Mostly, I was just happy we didn't personally know O.J. There was no need for us to do anything more than talk about his case over dessert.

***

The next day, I went into the store well after lunch. I knew Mikey could handle things. It seemed like a good idea to sleep late since I'd be staying up all night the very next day. In fact, I was tempted to spend the entire day in bed, but I did have to get a few things done at work.

Walking in, the first thing Mikey said to me was, "I've had six calls about *Wayne's World 2*."

This was a bone of contention. I'd ordered seven copies, but Mikey had insisted we needed at least ten. Sequels didn't always rent as well as the original, and if they didn't rent to the point of breaking even we'd end up with three or four extra copies floating around the store for years. I hated that.

I was about to thank him for the info, when the screeching sound of the modem made me jump. It was not my favorite noise. The damn thing sat on the counter next to the computer that recorded all our sales. The modem, which connected us to Prodigy, was touchy. It frequently stopped working and had to be restarted. It seemed that's what was going on just then.

Mikey was excited about creating an interweb page for us, though honestly, I wasn't sure why. I mean, if you wanted to rent a video you had to come to the store. If you wanted to ask a question, you could call us and talk to an actual living person. I couldn't quite see the point of an interweb page, other than to keep Mikey busy. Which did have its charms. And maybe he was right, maybe it was a good idea. The jury was still out on that one.

"Thanks for the info," I said, and went to hide in my office. On my desk I found two boxes of videos I had ordered. I opened them and checked to make sure I'd actually gotten what I ordered. I didn't always.

Five copies of *Ace Ventura: Pet Detective*—Mikey thought I should have gotten ten of that one too, but it looked terrible. Three copies of *The Pelican Brief*, two copies of *The Air Up There*, two copies of *The Piano*, one copy of *The Double Life of Veronique*, and six copies of *Dr. Doolittle*. Honestly, I wasn't excited about any of them.

I was halfway through putting the new videos into our system when Mikey popped in. "You have to come see this."

And then he was gone. I walked out to the front, sure he was going to explain something about the World Wide Web that I really didn't need to know. I already knew more about it than I wanted to. But when I got out to the counter, the TV above it had been tuned to KTLA, which was the only TV channel we got clearly. On the screen was a shot from a helicopter of a freeway. It seemed that one white vehicle was being followed by an entire freeway full of cars.

"Randy called to tell me. Can you believe it?"

"What is it?"

"A white Bronco. O.J. Simpson is inside."

"Okay."

I can't say that made any sense.

"He was supposed to turn himself in this morning, but he didn't. The police are going to arrest him."

"Is that a chase? I mean, it's kind of slow."

"He's in the Bronco with a friend. His friend is on the phone with the police. They're negotiating."

"They're what?"

"Negotiating."

"Um… They think he killed two people. They don't normally negotiate with suspected double murderers."

"He's O.J. They're not going to shoot him in the middle of the 5 freeway. There'd be another riot."

Okay, that did make sense.

The door opened and Eldridge Hall walked in to begin his shift. He was twenty years old, tall and angular, with dark brown hair and eyes. He almost always wore a black leather jacket and a collection of political pins. The smile on his face always made me happy to see him.

Like Marc and Lewis, he'd had a sunburn most of the week. Aside from a few flakes at the top of his forehead, the only remaining evidence was that his eyes were surrounded by white skin. He'd been wearing sunglasses most of that day and now looked a bit like an inverted raccoon.

"What's going on?" he asked, meaning the television we were staring at.

We repeated what the reporters had been saying.

"Wow, that's major."

Mikey was too enrapt to respond. This was my chance. I leaned in toward Eldridge and quietly said, "Could I talk to you in my office?"

I could have just asked him about the craft table in front of Mikey, but I didn't want Mikey to wonder why he wasn't being asked. Especially since I'd convinced myself Eldridge was probably going to say no. If I asked in front of Mikey and he said no, well, Mikey could yes and then… I didn't even want to think about that.

When we got back to my office I closed the door, which left

me standing very close to Eldridge. I cleared my throat and stepped behind my desk. I sat down and started playing with a pen.

"So, um, I have a question I want to ask you… You probably won't want to, so I want you to know it's okay to say—"

"Yes."

"Excuse me?"

"The answer's yes."

"I haven't asked the question."

"You kind of did."

"No, I kind of did not."

"You're asking me out, right?" There was uncertainty in his voice as he began to understand this might not be about what he thought it was about.

"Oh, um, actually, my friend Marc was on the show *Kapowie!*, which you might know already, and, anyway… They're shooting a reunion show on Saturday night. Like, overnight."

"Okay," he said, still looking confused because it did still sound like I was asking him on a kind of weird date, even though I wasn't.

"Anyway, Louis, who's Marc's partner—I know you know that, sorry—Louis is catering the craft table, which I'm helping him with, and we need someone else. To help. It's fifteen dollars an hour. It begins at eleven Saturday night and it lasts until seven Sunday morning. And I thought… you know, you could probably use the extra money. But now that I'm asking, I'm sure you have better—"

"Oh, um, yeah. I could." He looked crushed for a moment then rallied. "Saturday? Sure. I can do that."

"Great. Louis wants to meet in front of the store at ten."

"No problem."

I got up and started around my desk to open the door for him, but he said, "I can open the door."

"Of course, you can."

He walked out of the office and shut the door behind him. I felt just awful. And at the same time a bit elated. He'd said yes. He said he'd go out with me. Not that it could happen. Bad idea. Terrible idea. I shouldn't even think about it.

But I wasn't sure how to think about anything else.

TWO

"Oh my God, did I wake you?"

"Mmmmm, ggggrrrrrpppppp."

"What time is it there? I thought it was eleven... Oh, dear. It *is* eleven. And you have that *Kapowie!* thing tonight, don't you?"

"Hello, Mom."

She let a moment pass before she asked the question she'd called to ask.

"Are you excited?"

"Why would I be excited?" I couldn't help teasing her. I knew why she thought I'd be excited.

"Finn Henderson! You'll have to call me tomorrow and tell me everything. I mean, after you get some sleep—but definitely before Monday."

"Do you want an autograph?"

"No. Don't be silly."

She'd spent enough time with us in LA to know that approaching stars at all, no less for an autograph, was very uncool. I sat up in bed and tried to focus.

"I think Leon is crazy not to go with you guys."

"I think Leon is crazy."

She stifled a laugh, then said, "Crazy or not, he's a good friend and you know it."

Leon had recently done a deep background check on a Ford salesman named Rick Henley. On the surface at least, he seemed safe for my mother to date. He was just a bit older than she was, divorced but amicably. Or at least without restraining orders or accusations of abuse. His ex remarried almost immediately, so it seemed that if there was infidelity it was on her part. He still lived in the house they'd bought together in 1973. There was a four-year-old mortgage of about sixty percent of the value, so it appeared he'd bought his wife out. There were two adult children living outside of Michigan. According to my mother he was close with them, and Leon could find no reason to doubt that.

"How is Rick?"

"He's fine. We're having lunch again this week. He wants me to look at a red Thunderbird they just got in."

"Are you dating or buying a car?"

"I think we're dating, but if he tries to sell me a car then the dealership will pay for the lunch. He doesn't try very hard. Oh, and can you believe that I almost bought you a white Bronco?!"

Honestly, I did not remember that. She might have mentioned wanting to buy me a Bronco at one point. I don't think we actually got to the point of discussing color.

"Yeah, that's wild," I said. Sometimes it was best to just agree.

"Rick says that was the worst possible publicity for Ford. A slow-speed car chase really doesn't do much for a brand." Then she sighed and said, "Poor O.J."

"What about the people he probably killed?"

"Oh, I feel terrible about that, of course. But the worst is over for them. But O.J. ... They said he was holding a gun to his head. He was going to kill himself. I think he feels bad about what he did."

"That doesn't make it okay."

"I didn't say it was... Really Noah, I can feel bad for him if I want. He's going to spend the rest of his life in prison."

I really need coffee, I thought, right before my brain wandered off to weigh the question of which was better: a life in prison or death? Tough choice. And one I was glad I didn't have to make.

"Have you been getting out?" My mother asked.

"What do mean have I been getting out? I go to work every day."

"That's not what I meant."

"I had dinner with Marc and Louis on Thursday."

"That's in your front yard. That's not getting out. Have you been getting out into the world? Going places? Meeting people? Being *young*!"

"I went to the grocery store."

"You know that's not what I mean."

"I know what you mean."

In the last few years, I *had* gotten out into the world. I'd taken a photography class, which eventually led to a dead body in the dumpster behind my store. I joined a support group, which led to a dead body in my bed. And I'd taken a trip to Las Vegas, which led to a dead body on the roof of a car. Fortunately not my car, but you get the idea. Staying home seemed like the rational thing to do.

"You're going to just ignore me, aren't you?"

"Yup."

After the briefest pause, she said, "Well... You need to get some rest. You have quite the night in front of you. You can't spend the morning hanging on the phone."

"Yeah. Okay. Thanks for calling, Mom."

I rolled over and slept for another hour and a half.

I spent the afternoon doing this and that, mostly resisting the urge to call the store and check on things. Around seven, I finally took a shower and found myself staring in the mirror. I'd recently gone to an old-fashioned barber and had him buzz my hair off. I know I looked like a dishonorably discharged Marine, but it solved the issue of what to do with my hair. People said it made my eyes look bigger. I still wasn't sure if I liked it, but I did like the compliments. They were compliments, right?

Other than that, I was still the same big-eared, smallish, too-old-to-be-called-a-twink average gay guy. There was some bad news: I was getting crow's-feet. But there was also good news: I was getting old. Or at least older. For a long time, I hadn't been sure that would happen.

I'd gotten into an experimental trial for some new AIDS drugs, and they were working. My most recent blood test showed that my T-cells were increasing. Something they'd never done before. They'd dipped down to slightly less than three hundred at one point. Now they were almost five hundred. Just below normal. My doctor was really happy. I was really happy. It also felt weird.

Staring in the mirror like that, I began to feel like a movie character having an existential crisis. I brushed my teeth and went to get dressed. Then I spent part of the evening watching *Kapowie!*

The videos had recently been released due mainly to the deal with the Nostalgia Channel, which almost immediately became OTN—which stands for Old Time Network. Honestly, I didn't consider that an improvement.

Yes, I should probably have watched the show long before now. It had been in my store for at least three months. What can I say? I'm hardly the demographic. The episode I watched opened with all eight of the teens—four boys and four girls—singing and dancing in front of a multicolored, psychedelic backdrop. The song was something about how we're all sisters and brothers. Which frankly sounded incestuous.

At first, it was hard to pick out which kid was Marc. It was easy to pick out which teen was Finn Henderson, since photos of him on *Kapowie!* were often shown. Not to mention he was very nearly in his twenties when the show began. That left three boys as possible—oh, I found Marc.

Wow, he looked nothing like the man I knew. He was the youngest of the group, having barely started puberty. His face was round and cheeks full, as they still are. But his hair was long and thick, and cut into a shag. And he was skinny.

The clothes they wore to dance in were extreme: bell-bottoms with platform shoes. Two of the girls, Kathleen and Grace, wore shirts that exposed their midriff. Keely, the Black girl, had an exaggerated Afro. Even though it was almost twenty-years ago, I had the feeling they were all slightly out of step. They didn't look the way teenagers looked then; they looked the way adults thought teenagers looked then.

After the song, there was a sort of skit between Finn and Kathleen. It was a little story about a guy asking a girl if she wanted to go to the movies, except they did it three times. First, it was about how boys should *not* behave: Finn was sullen and monosyllabic. The date did not get made. The second time, it was about how girls should *not* behave: Kathleen was a flighty chatterbox who couldn't pay attention. The date did not get made. The third time, they each were articulate and listened to each other. The date got made. This was all accompanied by screen graphics that, rather than increase your understanding of the skit, just repeated what was clearly happening. BOYS ARE DUMB. GIRLS TALK TOO MUCH. LISTEN TO EACH OTHER.

The next section was Wes fixing a flat tire on his bike. I fast forwarded through that. There was another dance number, this time with just the girls. The song was about girls being just as smart as boys. The lyrics were kind of dumb though, so I wasn't sure if it was supposed to be a joke or just reinforce stereotypes. Then there was a scene that I assumed they'd be doing a version of every week. All the kids were at desks, as though in a classroom. But instead of having a class they each told jokes. It was sort of a take on the wall on *Laugh-In* from earlier in the seventies.

Marc stood out in this scene. He told jokes that were rip-offs of famous comedians. "I met my math teacher, Mrs. Josephs, in my pajamas. How she got in my pajamas I'll never know." There were ha-ha graphics on the screen to help you understand you were supposed to laugh. That was about all I could take. I rewound the tape and put it back into its plastic box.

Around nine-thirty, I went downstairs to see if I could help Louis. Even before I got to their front door, I could see that he'd been busy. There were two coolers already full of food. I peeked into one, it was filled to the brim with fruit. Next to that cooler was an industrial looking blender.

As I was gaping at the coolers, Louis came out of the house with a bag full of five dozen eggs. As he said hello, he began packing them into one of the coolers.

"What's the deal with the blender?"

"Oh, you don't know. The producers own ten juice bars in the valley, Juicy Juice franchises. I just got back from the one in North Hollywood. I had to pick up the blender and the cooler of fruit. The recipe book is in one of those bags."

He pointed to six Trader Joe's bags sitting next to his front door.

"Wow, this is a lot of stuff," I said.

"I know. We're going to have to figure out how four of us can carry it in one trip."

"One trip? Why? That doesn't make any sense. We're not going to just drive onto the lot?"

I'd been around enough studio people to know that if you worked there you called the guard and left what they call a drive-on, which meant you could park your car on the lot. Why wouldn't someone leave us a drive-on?

"Yeah, it's street parking only for some reason. We'll want to get everything into the studio in one trip."

"You know, I've never even heard of Bennett Day Studios before."

"They're pretty small. Five or six stages, I think. They started up after talkies, made a few movies themselves, but mostly they've been doing space rentals for decades. Indie productions. Overflow for the studios. Lots of commercial work. I went to their web page."

Louis was much more computer savvy than I was. Of course, I could have asked Mikey to do it, he'd have been thrilled.

"Should I bring some of these bags down to your car?"

"Thank you, that'd be great. We're taking Marc's car. It's bigger."

I grabbed three of the TJ bags by the handles, but then put one down as they were heavier than I expected. I brought those two bags down our newly painted red concrete steps and set them behind Marc's Infiniti. Then I went back upstairs. Louis was rearranging one of the two coolers to fit more stuff in.

"So... how many people are we feeding?"

"I was told fifteen."

"Which means..."

"I'm prepping for thirty."

"Oh my God."

I grabbed some more bags and brought them down to the car. Once we had everything down there, Louis began to load it in. The trunk took one of the coolers and a lot of the bags. The second cooler, the remaining bags, the blender and the thirty-cup coffeemaker went into the backseat. Rather than stacking everything in the middle, Louis put it all behind the driver—meaning that Eldridge and I were going to have to squeeze together very tightly all the way to Culver City.

"You know, I could bring my car," I said. I wanted to bring my car. That's why I had a car. To bring me places.

"Parking in Culver City is a nightmare," Marc said from behind me. He had a garment bag slung over his shoulder. He laid it on top of the things in the backseat. As he climbed into the front seat, I caught a closer glimpse of him.

"Are you wearing makeup?"

"I'm going to be on TV. Get in, we have to go."

I climbed into the backseat. My heart was beating a little faster than I liked and I was clammy. The last time I was in the backseat of a car I was being kidnapped. This situation was feeling uncomfortably similar. But that was silly. Marc and Louis were not kidnapping me. They weren't. They really weren't. Even if it felt like they were.

"Do you think we might finish early?" I asked.

Marc twisted around in his seat and stared at me like I was crazy. "That isn't even remotely a possibility."

"Great."

When we reached Pinx Video, Eldridge was standing out front. He was wearing an ACT-UP T-shirt, jean shorts and a pair of large work boots. He folded himself into the tiny space in the backseat with me, and we were off.

I was feeling anxious. Too anxious. And I couldn't figure out if my anxiety was coming from being pressed up against a cute boy or if it was the whole 'I was recently kidnapped' thing. Of course, it could have been both. A mix of sexual tension and abject terror.

"You're not wearing your leather jacket," I said to Eldridge's ear. A rather attractive ear, actually.

"Do you think I sleep in it or something?"

"No. I mean... No."

I *had* wondered if he slept in it. I mean, he wore it a lot.

"We're working. It'll get too hot and I'd have to put it somewhere safe. And I don't know that there will be somewhere safe. It seemed easier to not bring it."

"There's going to be a lot of actors," Marc said. "He's afraid one of them will steal it."

"I'm not."

"It's okay. One of them probably would."

We drove for a few blocks. I leaned in close to Eldridge—well, closer. I was already close. And whispered, "I am sorry about this. I did offer to drive."

"It's okay. I've had worse dates."

"It's not a date."

"Potato, potahto."

"Stop talking about vegetables. It's not a date."

He shrugged. A moment later, we made a turn rather sharply and the two of us were pressed even closer together. I'm sure we looked like something out of the porno section at Pinx.

Except, you know, with clothes.

THREE

Bennett Day Studios was on Washington Boulevard west of the Sony lot. It was composed of five soundstages and six or seven other smaller buildings all behind a ten-foot wall. It had two entrances, one to the north on Washington and one to the south on Culver. The 405 was so close it was nearly a part of the studio. The surrounding streets were mostly residential, which meant parking was terrible since some of them, most of them, required permits. It was a small studio, so they might not have had much in the way of their own parking. Though since it was nighttime, I thought there really should have been some available.

Their gate was not nearly as ornate as the larger studios. In fact, it was kind of bland. It was black iron and only large enough for one truck to pass through. Next to it was a small guard's hut with a pedestrian door beside it.

Inside the guard's hut was an overweight White guy of about forty, probably older. He was scanning the street, which I suppose was actually his job. He was supposed to be making sure nothing illegal was happening. And as nearly as I could tell, nothing illegal was happening.

When we pulled up, there were two limousines double-parked on either side of the gate. Eight people were standing on the nearby sidewalk: five women and three men. One of the men was a balding, husky, bearded guy in his early thirties standing apart from the rest, with several cases of what looked like camera equipment. He wore a dark T-shirt under a flannel shirt.

Even as Louis double-parked the Infiniti between the limos, he managed to growl and say, "Mmmmm... bear crossing."

"I saw," said Marc.

I was used to this behavior, though mostly it took place during beer busts at leather bars. It seldom happened in the 'wild' as it were.

I said to Eldridge, who was still practically on top of me. "They do that."

"They like bears. I get it."

The car stopped moving. I immediately peeled myself off Eldridge and got out to start unpacking. Well, I tried to. From the group, a woman in her late fifties hurried over to us—well, to me as it turns out—saying, "Marc! My goodness, you haven't changed a bit!" I have to admit I jumped a little.

In her early sixties, she was a once-natural blonde who kept her hair in one long, thick, graying braid. Her clothes were black and flowing, a long skirt and a shapeless top. She was a bit breathless, as though she'd run a long distance rather than a few feet.

"My name's Noah. I'm helping out with the craft table."

"Wendy, I'm over here," Marc said. He already had an extra-long cigarette in his hand and was waving it around like Cruella de Ville.

"Oh! Ha! Silly me." She set down the bag she was holding and hurried over to hug Marc. I can't say he looked too pleased. When she let him go, she said, "I've got a Polaroid camera in my bag. We'll get a photo later. I promised your mother."

"My mother?!"

Quickly, to avoid his agitation, she turned to me, saying, "You must be Louis."

"I just said, 'I'm Noah.'"

"Oh, so you did. I'd forget my head if it wasn't attached. I'm sorry. *Noah*."

Over her shoulder, I watched Marc. He was smoking angrily. In the years that I've known him I couldn't remember him saying much about his parents, other than they were disappointed he didn't become a major movie star.

"*I'm* Louis," Louis said, busily making piles of TJ's bags and coolers on the curb.

Wendy held out the Trader Joe's bag she carried, saying, "I'm Wendy. Nice to finally meet you. I brought cups from our store. When you make—"

"Great. We've got a lot to carry, though. Could you walk those in for us?" Louis asked. "And... nice to meet you too. In person."

"Of course, yes." Turning around, she called out, "Donald, come meet Louis. Donald..."

"I'm actually busy just now," Louis said, far too politely. "Can we do that inside?"

"Oh, well, yes, of course..." She wandered off calling out, "Donald... never mind... Donald..."

Marc had the look of a thunderstorm—or that might have been the cloud of smoke he'd worked up.

Louis took one look and said, "Oh my. I think I need to park the car." Then, "Eldridge, if you could take that cooler and the bag on top. Noah, if you'd take those five bags. They're not as heavy as they look."

That left a cooler and two bags for Louis. Knowing Louis, they were the heaviest bags and the heaviest cooler. He was like that.

"I'll be back in a minute," he said, before jumping back into the car. Leaving me alone with Marc.

"I guess Wendy knows your mom," I said, unable to tamp down my curiosity.

"I was thirteen when the show started. My parents were around a lot. I didn't know she *still* knew them."

I had the feeling the photograph was not going to happen.

Just then, a Black woman a few years older than Marc and I broke away from the others and came over. Like the others, she had a garment bag hung over her arm. She had also wrangled two huge floral arrangements onto the sidewalk. They were at least two and a half-feet tall with spikey flowers shooting out in all directions. She left them where they were on the sidewalk and hurried over.

"Marc! Oh my God. You haven't changed at all!"

Which was interesting, because she was actually talking to Marc and not me. I'd seen the show and been mistaken for Marc, so I had to admit… he had changed. A lot.

"Keely!" he practically squealed. They were hugging, as two other women came over. A short, heavyset, nerdy-looking woman, whose name turned out to be Meg, and another who was sharply dressed and looked vaguely familiar. Marc saw them and gave another squeal and then there were hugs all around.

"Can you believe we're doing this?" Meg said. She was talking very fast. "It's so weird that we're all together again, isn't it? Except for Wes, I mean. He's not coming. Did Donald tell you? Do you know anything about that? Did you keep in touch with him?"

"No, I didn't," Marc said. "I think I heard something about him backpacking in Europe."

"I heard he went to prison," Keely said.

"No! Where did you hear that?"

"If it was in one of the tabloids," the familiar-looking woman said, "it can't possibly be true. If it were true we'd have to believe that aliens are running our government."

Meg giggled. Though I did think she had a point.

"I don't read those, so I wouldn't have heard it there," Keely said before changing the subject. "Marc, how are your mom and dad? They were so sweet."

"I don't know. I don't see them."

Keely took a breath, and said, "Oh, thank God, they were horrible. I always felt sorry for you."

"You felt sorry for me? *I* felt sorry for me."

Donald hovered nearby. In his early sixties, he was bald with bushy eyebrows sitting too high above his eyes. He looked like he'd raised them in surprise and they'd never come back down. He held a clipboard in his hand.

"Okay, so that was Louis," he said, pointing to the Infiniti, which was slowly cruising for a parking space well down the block, then making a check on his clipboard. "And Marc." Who was paying no attention to him and was instead asking the girls— Meg, Keely and *Grace*—about themselves. Donald made another check. Then to me, "And you are?"

"Noah Valentine."

"Helper number one." Check.

"Eldridge Hall."

"Helper number two." Check. Then, sounding like a school principal, he said, "Louis needs to hurry back. We're going in all together at exactly eleven. Nine minutes. No stragglers."

I wasn't sure what he wanted us to do. We couldn't make it easier for Louis to park.

"He'll be back. He's very responsible," Marc said, breaking away from the girls and looking annoyed.

"Who's missing?" Wendy asked. "Is anyone else missing?"

"No one, we're all here," Donald said.

"Are you sure?"

"I can count, you know."

I reminded myself that Wendy and Donald were married to each other. Something about their demeanor drove that point home. They were obviously a team. Not a well-functioning team, but a team nonetheless.

"Is this what you were expecting?" Eldridge asked.

"I don't know. I don't know what I was expecting," I said, honestly. "It's a little chaotic I suppose."

"I think herding cats is the phrase you're looking for."

The only two not huddled around Marc were Ricky Bellows of the sex tape and the bearish bald guy with the camera equipment. Ricky wore a pair of jeans, a tank top that showed off his deeply muscled arms, and a gym bag slung over his shoulder. He looked like a thousand guys coming out of the gay gyms on Santa Monica Boulevard. If it weren't for an entitled swagger and a complete lack of grace, you'd think he was gay.

"Fabulous," Wendy said, looking at her watch. "We've got seven minutes."

"Sweetheart," Donald said, making the word sharp and unpleasant. "I just said nine."

"My watch says seven."

He looked at his watch and said, "Well, now my watch says eight. We synchronized before we left the house."

"Yes, I remember. I don't forget *everything*, you know."

"I wasn't saying you don't remember; I'm saying now we're off. How did we get off?"

"Your watch is obviously slow."

"Or yours is fast."

"My mobile phone says ten-fifty-three," Grace said. "Seven minutes. Speaking of which, I'm assuming reception is going to be crap inside?"

"The stages are made of concrete and rebar," Donald said. "I can't imagine you'll get much of a signal."

"Who are you going to call at this time of night, Grace?" Marc asked.

"I have clients."

"You're a real estate agent, dear, not a hooker," Marc told her. "If your clients are calling at eleven at night—"

"Ten-fifty-four."

"If they're calling this late, you shouldn't answer."

Donald then said to his wife, "Can you start getting people in line. I'll deal with... this." He motioned toward the limousines.

It didn't take much to figure out that Finn Henderson was in one of the limos while Kathleen True was in the other.

Despite the fact that they were in different parts of the entertainment business, they were both stars deserving of star treatment.

Donald walked over to the first limousine and tapped on the window. Before the window opened, a woman wearing a mannish black suit jumped out of the second limousine and hurried over.

A voice from inside the first limo said, "My mom doesn't want to go in until everyone has gone first. Someone needs to show us directly to her dressing room."

"I'm Amber Bright. Mr. Henderson's manager," the woman said, tapping Donald on the shoulder. "Mr. Henderson is going in last. And he'll need to go directly to his dressing room. No one's to speak to him, I want that understood. And please, don't look him in the eye."

"No one should speak to my mom either," said the voice inside the limo. "And *she* goes in last."

"They can't both go in last unless they go in together," Donald said.

Immediately, Amber and the voice screamed "No!"

"Absolutely not."

"That can't happen."

"The thing is," Donald said, "We're all going in at the same time. That's what the studio has agreed to. How about if Finn is first in line and Kathleen is last. Would that work? And you need to decide really fast because we're going in four minutes from now. Or three. Or five. Something like that."

It was really Amber's decision, or rather Finn's. After a moment, she sighed deeply and said, "Oh, all right, fine. If Kathleen's going to *insist*. Mr. Henderson just wants to be reasonable."

Someone said something deep in the limo, and then the voice said, clearly repeating it, "My mom's a Christian. Christians are *always* reasonable."

Most of us were close enough to overhear the exchange.

Eldridge stood next to me and quietly said, "He can't really believe that, can he?"

"No one expects the Spanish Inquisition," Marc said, quoting Monty Python. "Just one example of Christian reasonableness."

"Salem witch trials," Eldridge countered.

"The Crusades."

"Centuries of British history."

"Okay guys, that's enough," I whispered. "Your point was made, and he wouldn't believe you anyway."

Amber walked away from the limo and its window rose. Behind us, Ricky asked loudly, "We could bring people? Donald, you said we couldn't. My girlfriend really wanted to come. Why do they get to bring people?"

Donald ignored him. "If we could form a line. Quickly."

Wendy hadn't actually encouraged us to do that. Now that we knew Finn would be going in first, Ricky, Meg and Keely hurried over to get into the second spot. Ricky won the race.

Grace offered to take a bag. She had a wardrobe bag slung over one arm. Marc said, "I'm sorry, I should have introduced you all. Noah, Eldridge... this is Grace Horlock."

"Oh, the real estate agent," I blurted, finally recognizing her. "I've seen your picture on lawn signs. And bus stops."

"Then you must be spending your time in some very ritzy neighborhoods."

I hadn't thought about that, but the houses she offered were usually on the tops of hills around the city.

"Louis and I are looking for a house," Marc said. "We'll have to talk."

"I don't speak to anyone with less than a million to spend. But for you I'll make an exception."

"How would you know if—" Marc started.

"Please, I can tell a person's net worth at a glance." She turned to me and said, "So sorry, dear."

"What? No. Wait." She was right that I couldn't afford to buy a house, but I wouldn't say I deserved pity.

Then Finn Henderson stepped out of his limo. He was wearing a pair of impenetrable aviators. Sunglasses at night were a very LA thing. They screamed 'I'm important, notice me but don't look at me.' He had a square jaw, cheekbones that looked carved from stone, and artfully messy chocolate-colored hair. As everyone knows, beneath the glasses were intense, brilliant blue eyes. In a nod to Frank Sinatra—Ol' Blue Eyes—the press often called Finn 'Young Blue Eyes.' Clunky, I know.

Seemingly satisfied that Finn had gotten out first, Kathleen True left her limo. She, too, wore a pair of sunglasses, giant and white-rimmed, along with a colorful scarf on her head. She wore a shiny black fur coat and carried a hat box in one hand. Even mostly covered, you could tell she was a beautiful woman—though she looked more like a fifties' movie star than an evangelist's wife.

Getting out of the limo behind her was her fourteen-year-old adopted son, Heston True. He wore nothing but black, had dyed his hair so it was a lifeless soot color, he'd put on a ridiculous amount of mascara—and obviously never went into the sun. Clearly, he and his parents were having issues.

Over one shoulder he'd slung a black backpack. In one hand, he carried what was clearly his mother's makeup, in the other he struggled to keep a garment bag from dragging along the ground. I wondered if his mother knew the difference between a child and a pack mule.

Finn and Kathleen studiously avoided looking at each other as they took their places at the front and rear of the line. Well, it seemed like they didn't look at each other. Behind their sunglasses, their eyes could have been doing almost anything.

"Dude, it's so good to see you," Ricky said to Finn, only to be ignored. Apparently, Amber had been serious when she laid down the 'don't talk to him' rule.

"Two minutes," Wendy said.

Louis was still not back.

Seriously, it was like a space launch. I didn't see the big deal, but we all did as we were told. I picked up four bags, two in each hand. We got in line. Then Eldridge went over and got the cooler and bag Louis would carry in when he got there. His own cooler sat in front of him.

I heard Meg saying to Keely, "Your flowers are beautiful, but... I hope you know foxglove is poisonous."

"Of course, I know that. *All* florists know that. But they're only poisonous if you *eat* them. I don't think anyone's going to eat them. Do you?"

I got a squidgy feeling in my stomach. I really should have stayed home. She was right. No one was going to eat the poisonous flowers. But I didn't need reminding that the world was a dangerous place and that someone could accidentally eat a flower and end up—

"I'm not carrying that, Donald. You know I'm not supposed to lift anything heavy," Wendy said.

I glanced over. The bearish guy was carrying a heavy looking case and a bag. Donald had a camera bag slung over his shoulder and three cloth Juicy Juicy shopping bags.

"It's not that heavy," Donald said.

"I think I get to decide what is and is not heavy. That's heavy."

"I've seen you carry twenty pounds of fruit, Wendy."

"Watch your step," she hissed.

We all did our best to look elsewhere. Searching the street, looking for Louis seemed like a good idea. We studied each direction. Nothing.

"What happens if Louis doesn't get here in time?" I asked.

No one said a word. That was ominous. Then, at the back of the line, Kathleen said, "Can't we just go in? I don't stand on street corners."

We weren't exactly on a corner, so I didn't see—

And then, finally, Louis ran up to join us. Donald nodded at the guard, who came around and opened the door. He was looking over his shoulder, seemingly worried someone might see our little parade. We were ushered in single file through the door and onto the lot. Donald kept whispering that we needed to be quiet.

I hoped we didn't have to walk far. Others had taken some of the bags, but I still had three to deal with. Plus, the whole thing was ridiculous. I felt like we were the Von Trapp family attempting to escape the Nazis. And I wasn't the only one who felt that way. In front of me, Louis began to hum "Edelweiss."

FOUR

Stage 2 was roughly four hundred feet onto the lot. We entered by climbing three concrete steps and squeezing through a narrow door. That put us in a kind of tiny antechamber facing another door. Ricky was trying to talk to Finn about the Dodgers, who had apparently just beat the Reds. Marc was asking Louis where he found parking.

And then, thankfully, we were beyond that. Someone flipped a switch somewhere and basic lighting came on. Directly in front of us was a long hallway that looked as though it ran the length of the soundstage. To our left was a door about ten feet away. It opened onto the stage itself. I couldn't see much, just a sliver of a brightly colored set.

"Do you know what they shoot here?" I asked.

A couple of people nearby shrugged. The bearish guy said, "*Guessmate?.*"

I've never seen *Guessmate?*, have you? From the commercials I assume it's a game show having something to do with two teams of two—one celebrity, one normal, everyday human being—answering silly, barely logical questions, and then making their way across a projected checkerboard à la Pac-Man without getting trapped by the other team. How all that comes together I've never been interested enough to find out.

Donald turned around to face us and said, "Wendy, would you take Mr. Henderson and Ms. Bright down to the Zola Emery dressing room? It's at the far end of the hallway. I'll take Mrs. True and her son to the Fatty Arbuckle dressing room, the first door on our left. Meg and Keely, you're in Barrymore. Marc and Grace in Cagney. And Ricky, you're on your own in Durante."

That was all very confusing. The dressing rooms were named after actors? Actors from a million years ago? Ones no one remembers? Zola Emery and Fatty Arbuckle were from the silent era. We didn't even have any of their videos at Pinx.

Donald picked out Louis, and said, "There's a craft room halfway down. You can prep in there. You'll find a banquet table against one wall. If you could bring that out and set up in front of the risers—thanks so much."

Then, "Ed, if you could bring the camera equipment onto the set that would be great." Apparently, Ed was the name of the bearish guy.

Before we began moving, Grace asked, "Is there a makeup person coming? Hair?"

"If you need any help with that sort of thing Wendy will lend a hand." Donald said, before saying, "Right this way, Mrs. True."

"If I have time I'll help, of course," Wendy sniped. "I *am* being stretched a little thin."

Grace frowned, and said, "Seriously? No makeup? No hair? No wardrobe?"

"What did you expect, Grace?" Meg said. "We always did the show on a shoestring. Did you really think this would be different?"

"I know but... we at least had Melvin. Yes, they made him do everything, but he was fabulous. I was kind of hoping he'd be here to comb out my hair."

I can't say that made a lot of sense. Her hair looked fine. Great even. And her makeup—

"Don't worry, I'll help you," Meg said.

"I'm not letting you touch my hair."

"It was just an offer."

Louis led Marc, Eldridge and me down the hallway. We struggled with the coolers and the bags and the giant industrial blender, but I was still able to get a peek at the Arbuckle room, which was large and had some furniture in addition to the makeup table, giant mirror and chairs. Keely had already dropped off one of the enormous floral arrangements, which took up half of the table. Donald was fawning over Kathleen True and her son. Neither of them seemed to be paying attention. In fact, Heston was already on the couch deep into his Gameboy.

Next to it, the Barrymore room—there were brass signs on each of the doors—was still empty and not nearly as roomy. There was the makeup table, chairs and not much else. Then there was another empty dressing room just like it, the Cagney room. Just as Donald said, the craft room was in the middle—it was not named after anyone. Probably because it wasn't much more than a counter, an ice machine, a folded banquet table against one wall, and a huge sink. It had two lights on the ceiling, one of them was flickering.

After we set down the bags and coolers, I asked Marc, "Are you okay?"

"I'm fine. There's nothing to worry about."

"Oh God, I know that tone of voice," Louis said. "There's a lot to worry about. What's going on?"

Marc rolled his eyes. "It's just the thing with my parents. People keep bringing them up. That's all. Not a big deal. We just have to get through tonight and everything will be fine."

He tried to give Louis a reassuring smile, saying, "All right, I'm going to get ready now."

Louis kissed him. "Good luck, dear."

"Thank you, I think I might be needing it."

As soon as Marc was gone, Louis said to us, "I'm going to get the coffee urn going." He pointed at the ancient, two-foot-tall metal coffee pot sitting on the counter. Then he noticed me staring at the five pound can of bargain brand coffee he'd pulled out of a bag. "Don't worry, I've got a trick up my sleeve." He put the urn into the sink and started filling it with cold water.

"I know Marc's parents wanted him to be a movie star. Is that all that's going on?"

"They wanted him to be a movie star so they could have the money. They took most of what he made as a kid."

"That's not legal," Eldridge said.

"While he was a minor, they had to put something like twenty percent into a trust. The rest they got to spend... supposedly on taking care of him. When Marc was eighteen, they basically coerced him into giving them the money from the trust. He managed to keep enough to get an AA in accounting, but they got their hands on the rest."

"Was it a lot of money?"

"Well, we'd probably be in a house already."

"Oh. I guess that's why his parents are never around for the holidays."

"You're so lucky to have Angie." Then to Eldridge he said, "She's going to love you."

"Louis!"

"What? I'm sure you'll bring her around to the store next time she's here."

I blushed deeply. Louis lifted the urn out of the sink and set it on the table. He filled the basket with the can of cheap ground coffee. Then he took a bottle of cinnamon and shook in two or three tablespoons. Or maybe teaspoons. I don't know, but it was a lot.

He glanced at us and said, "Works like a charm. Can you two take that folding table out and set it up in front of the risers like Donald said?"

"Okay." I grabbed one end of the table while Eldridge grabbed the other. We walked back by the Cagney room. Its door was open, and I could see Grace and Marc sitting in front of the mirror chatting. Next was the Barrymore room, where Keely and Meg were getting ready. Things in there looked a little chilly. The door to the Arbuckle room was shut, though I could still hear Donald's fawning voice. Even without words it sounded like he was giving undeserved compliment after undeserved compliment.

Eldridge said, "You know this place is haunted, don't you?"

"What? Why would I know that?"

"Everyone knows that. Haven't you ever been on that haunted Hollywood tour?"

"No."

"Oh, well maybe we should—"

"No."

"Anyway, Zora Emery hung herself in one of the dressing rooms. Probably the one named after her. She was making her first talkie and, well, I guess it wasn't going well. People claim they hear her voice late at night. Rehearsing her lines."

"Is it a grating voice?" I couldn't help asking.

"Very."

"You don't really believe in ghosts."

"No. But I do believe in stories about old Hollywood."

"You really like that stuff, don't you?"

"Um... why do you think I work in a video store?"

He had a point. It certainly wasn't for the money I was paying him. Then he asked, "So... Marc and Louis are a cute couple. You've known them a while, I guess?"

"I met them when I moved into the apartment above theirs. I guess it's been about three years."

"Mikey says you're all best friends."

"We are."

"Good friends means good people."

"Yeah... not always. The Hillside Stranglers were good friends *and* cousins."

Eldridge frowned at me. "Really? You just compared yourself and your friends to a couple of serial killers."

"Well..." Changing the subject seemed to be the best option. "How about we put the table right over... here."

Just then, someone, probably Ed, turned the stage lights on. The set behind us was shockingly bright. I glanced upward, and above the risers I saw that there was some kind of control room. I could see a silhouette through the window but not who it was.

After a moment I went back to the table; I wasn't there to gawk. We unfolded the banquet table and spread a giant table-cloth over it—a floral black-and-white print. It was actually too big, so I used a trick Louis had shown me where you tie a simple knot into each corner to make the cloth smaller.

"Is Louis a caterer?"

"No. He's in IT."

"Why does he have such a big tablecloth?"

"Because he's Louis."

I was quite used to Louis going into the tiny apartment he shared with Marc and coming out with whatever was needed in any given situation. That he could cater snacks and an early morning breakfast for fifteen out of his personal belongings didn't strike me as odd.

After the comments Eldridge made in the car, and the comments Marc and Louis kept making, I decided I really ought to set things straight. "Eldridge, you know that I'm your boss."

"Tonight?"

"Well, no. Tonight Louis is your boss."

"Okay. So you're not my boss."

"What I mean is... I really *can't* ask you out. Because I'm your boss."

"But you're not my boss tonight."

"No, not tonight. I'm trying to explain—"

"That you *can* ask me out tonight."

"No. I mean, I'm still your boss—"

"But not right now."

"I'm still your boss in the larger sense. And that prevents me from—"

"So *I* could ask *you* out?"

"You could… I just can't accept."

"Because you're my boss. In the larger sense."

"Yes, that's right."

Thank goodness that was over, I thought just before he said, "If I quit, can you go out with me?"

"Oh my God, don't quit. We love—Mikey really likes you."

"You don't like me?"

"You're doing an excellent job at the store and I'd hate to lose you."

"Not even if that meant we could go on a date?"

I didn't get a chance to answer because Louis was there carrying a plastic tub filled with the snacks.

"Okay, I've started the coffee. And I brought an electric kettle for hot water in case anyone wants tea."

At that point, I realized there were no electrical outlets anywhere near where we'd put the table. Would we need one? There were cables running all over the stage. If we needed one, maybe—

"Noah, find something to write on and check with everyone to see who wants coffee and how they want it. The cream and sugar are next to the coffeemaker, as are the Styrofoam cups. If anyone wants tea, we have Constant Comment, which has caffeine, and Lemon Zinger, which does not. I dumped ice into the sink and put a bunch of sodas and evian in it to get cold. There's a tray in there, you'll see it. I'm going to keep Eldridge here to help me set up the table."

"Okay. Where do you think I'll find something to write on?"

"I think there's an office down past the dressing rooms."

"Unlocked?"

"Hopefully."

I went back to the dressing rooms and then down the long hallway. It's a very weird feeling to start work at eleven at night. It feels out of step with the rest of the world, and at the same time dramatic and a little exciting. Well, I *was* helping to make television. That was exciting. Or rather, I was feeding people who were making television. That seemed less exciting.

The smell of coffee brewing didn't help with the strangeness, though. Coffee suggested morning. It was definitely not morning, given the way my eyes were starting to droop. I wondered again if this was a big mistake. No, no, it was not a mistake. The worst thing that would happen was that I'd take a break in one of the audience seats and fall asleep. Maybe I'd snore and get made fun of when I woke up. That's all. That's the worst. I needed to relax.

When I got to the office—which had D.W. Griffith's name on the door—it was a cramped little room with a desk, a chair and a telephone. I found a pen in the top drawer but nothing to write on. I popped into the men's room—thankfully unnamed—and grabbed a paper towel. The pen worked. Going back down the hallway, I was about to knock on the door of the Emery room when I heard Amber saying sharply, "You can't fire me. We have a contract."

I decided I'd come back later. I went further down the hall and walked through the open door to the Durante room. Ricky Bellows sat in front of the mirror making faces at himself. On the table in front of him were a number of makeup products, mainly bronzer. He'd taken off his tank top and seemed to have little interest in putting on anything else. His chest was impressive. I tried not to think about that, and said, "Hi. Can I get you a cup of coffee?"

He gave me a curious look and I thought he was about to ask me something like, did we have Sweet'N Low, which made me realize I hadn't checked and I really should have. But instead, he said, "You guys are all fags, right?"

"Excuse me?"

"Marc and that older guy, Louis? And then the one in the fag T-shirt. You're all fags."

That was offensive. A lot. I chose to ignore it, and said, "I'm really just here to ask if you want coffee. And if so, did you want cream and sugar?"

"Don't get your tits in a twist. I'm okay with fags. I own three gyms. If I had a problem with fags I'd be out of business."

"That's so kind of you," I said, meaning the exact opposite. "Coffee? Milk? Sugar?"

"Naw, I don't want any coffee."

"Tea?"

He shook his head.

"A pop?" I offered.

"Lemme know when the Juicy Juice starts. I'm gonna want a Banana Blast."

"Will do."

I walked out of his dressing room deciding I'd be avoiding him as much as possible, when I found myself face to face with Amber Bright.

"Did I hear you mention soda? Is there Diet Coke?"

"I can get you one."

"It's right here, isn't it?" she said, pointing to the nameless craft room.

"Yeah…" I turned and we walked into the room. I was relieved to find Louis had put some Diet Coke on ice, though it would hardly be cold.

"Yeah, it's right here."

Amber breezed by me and grabbed a can of pop. Feeling that it was still warm, she also picked up a cup and scooped up some ice.

"Do you think Mr. Henderson would like coffee or a Coke?"

"What he wants is a speedball, but I'll bring him a Diet Coke."

FIVE

So far, I hadn't had to get anyone anything. I went out and walked down to the Cagney room. I knocked and heard Marc say, "Come in."

I went in as Grace was asking, "What's your price point?" She stared at herself in the mirror adding mascara to her already mascaraed eyelashes.

"Around three hundred thousand."

Grace's mouth dropped open. "Oh, you poor thing! Well, you won't have a pool. Or a view. Or very many rooms. But I'm sure your agent will find you something. Definitely in the flats, but with good bones, as they say. Although sometimes that just means it's unlikely to fall down."

"I think what you do is fascinating," Marc said.

"I love it! You know, I worked with this agent from William Morris. Sold him a cute little bungalow halfway up a hill in the Cahuenga Pass. Anyway, he told me the next big thing is going to be reality TV, like *Real World* except different. All these new cable channels need cheap programming. And so... I started to have this idea. And I'm thinking about it and thinking about it... And when I was selling Finn's last house and buying his new one —up near Mulholland—anyway, I pitched Finn my idea. He does have a production company, after all. Anyway, it was about a high-end real estate agent—me, in case you can't figure that out —selling properties in Beverly Hills. Basically, just having a camera follow me around."

I had no idea why that would be interesting, but Marc said, "Oh my God, I'd so watch that."

"Well, apparently, you're the only one. Finn said it was the stupidest thing he'd ever heard. Really hurt my feelings. Very unkind. I mean, no one wants to be told their life is too boring for TV. Especially given some of the things they put on."

"Exactly."

I thought I'd better ask my question and not just stand there listening. "Do you guys want coffee or a pop?"

"Coffee, please!" Marc said. "By the gallon."

"Cream and sugar?"

"Tons."

"Do you have nonfat milk?" Grace asked.

"No. It's real cream."

"Real cream? Are you trying to kill us?"

"Um... no."

"I'll play it safe with a Diet Coke."

"Coming right up," I said, leaving the room. I supposed I could have moved on and gotten more orders, but I was right there, so I popped back into the craft services room and made Marc's super sweet coffee and grabbed Grace's diet pop. I did use the tray, because I also brought her a cup of ice.

Back in their dressing room, Grace was saying, "Yes, I've bought and sold several houses for Finn, and I even handled a sale for Kathleen. Now, if you talk to either of them, I wouldn't mention the other. There's still a lot of bad blood."

"So, they really were dating toward the end of the show?" Marc asked.

"The end? No. All along. You don't remember?"

"I was a fourteen-year-old closet case. I was paying attention to other things."

"Like Melvin, as I recall."

"Nothing happened between us."

"So you say."

"He used to give me cigarettes. That's it."

"Anyway, I *was* paying attention and, yes, Finn and Kathleen were hot and heavy. I was shocked when she married Reverend True just months after the show ended... basically on the rebound. I had no idea she was religious. I suppose we should have known though... She's the one who had Melvin fired. For being a bad influence on you."

"Really? I thought it was my parents."

"Even if it was your parents, she was still behind it. She was a nightmare long before she got on Christian TV. She was just more subtle about it."

As I set their drinks down on the makeup table, Marc said, "Maybe it wasn't love with the good reverend. Maybe it was just good casting."

Grace squealed. "You're terrible! I love it!"

Unfortunately, I couldn't just stand there listening to their conversation. Marc would have to fill me in later. I left the dressing room and went on to the next one, the Barrymore room. The door was open, but I tapped on it anyway. Meg and Keely were intent on their make-up, not saying anything.

"Can I get either of you coffee or a pop?"

"Coffee. Black," Meg said. Then she glanced at Keely and looked embarrassed.

Keely noticed and shook her head, as she said, "Nothing for me, thanks."

I popped down to the Arbuckle room and knocked. The door opened a crack, and I was looking at Heston True's blue eyes through clumpy eyelashes. "Yeah?"

"Would you or your mom like coffee or pop?"

"I'll have coffee. Cream and sugar."

"No, he won't," Kathleen said from deeper into the room. I could only see a sliver of her at the makeup table. She'd put on a giant wig, which must have been what was in the hat box. It was almost lavender and looked more like something a drag queen would wear than a supposedly devout woman. "We'll have soda. Do you have anything without caffeine?"

"I think there's 7-Up."

"We'll have two of those, thank you."

"7-Up isn't going to keep me awake," Heston said.

"You can take a nap. You're not going to be on camera. Not looking like that, at least."

"I'm not sleeping on that sofa, Kathleen, it's gross," Heston said, as he shut the door in my face.

Through the door I heard her saying loudly, "Don't call me by my first name. I'm your mother. You're supposed to call me Mom."

I didn't hear him say anything. I did hear the beeping and popping of his Gameboy so he must have just ignored her.

I went to get their drinks. In the craft room, I filled a couple of cups with ice. As I did, I heard noises coming from the *Guessmate?* set. I could definitely hear Wendy's voice, though not much more than the occasional "Donald!" Apparently, the soundstage itself was soundproofed against the outside world, but the interior walls were paper thin. I wondered if that explained why people thought they sometimes heard Zola Emery practicing her lines? I could also hear music—which didn't make much sense. Had someone turned on a radio?

I filled a cup with black coffee for Meg and put everything on a tray, then walked back out into the hallway. Something moved and I looked down the hallway to see Ricky walking away from me. I was pretty sure I'd noticed bathrooms down that way. He must be going to the restroom. He really should have put a shirt on.

Marc and Grace were still chatting away as I walked by. The door to the Barrymore room was open, so I walked in and set Meg's coffee on the makeup table.

"So, who are you?" she asked.

"I'm a friend of Marc and Louis. I live in their building."

"And Louis is Marc's boyfriend?"

"He's doing the craft table."

"Don't let Kathleen know about them. She says terrible things about the gays on her show. That they're immoral, disease-ridden, AIDS-infected, devil-worship—"

"I'm aware. Thanks."

"She's probably still a racist, too," Keely said. "Though I'll bet she doesn't have the nerve to say anything against Black folk on TV."

Smiling, I said, "Well, I have to bring the racist a pop now."

That made them both giggle, which they quickly stopped when they realized the other found it funny. I left their dressing room and tapped on the door of the Arbuckle room again.

Heston opened it. This time he stepped back to allow me access. This dressing room was larger than the others, and it had its own private bathroom through a door to the left. My guess was the Emery room, which Finn was in, also had a private bathroom. Finn and Kathleen were both being given the star treatment.

Still, on closer inspection, the brown tweedy sofa looked filthy. I could see why Heston didn't want to sleep on it. But that didn't stop him from flopping onto it and going back to his Gameboy. The gigantic floral arrangement had been relegated to a spot on the floor, since Kathleen needed the space for her makeup case filled with massive amounts of makeup and hair products to style her wig.

As I set the pops down on the makeup counter, I couldn't help but look up at the ceiling. There were no pipes or beams. Nothing to hang yourself from. I wanted to take a peek into the bathroom. Did it have a shower? Could you hang yourself from a showerhead? Were things different in the Emory room? How had Zola Emery killed herself?

"Uh-hum," Kathleen cleared her throat. "I asked you a question."

"Oh. Sorry. What was it?"

"How does Finn look? Does he look... high?"

"Someone else brought him a pop, so I wouldn't know."

"Hmmmm..." she said, as though that meant something. "Supposedly, he's been to rehab and he's sober. But then, Finn has never been particularly honest. If you think he's still using, you *will* come and tell me."

It wasn't a question or a request, it was a command. The simplest way to get out of the room was to say, "Sure thing."

As I came out of the Arbuckle room shutting the door behind me, I was about to turn to go out to the stage, but Marc was suddenly there. In his hand was an etched silver cigarette case, probably antique. He held it out, saying, "Look what I found in the drawer of my makeup table."

"Do you think it belonged to Jimmy Cagney?"

"No. It's mine."

"Finders keepers."

"No, it *really* is mine. From when I was fourteen."

"Wait. You smoked when you were fourteen?"

"Not the point. I *lost* this case when I was fourteen."

"Sorry, I'm still—you were a fourteen-old-smoker who used a cigarette case?"

"Still not the point. The point is someone's had it all this time. They left it there for me to find."

"Why not just give it to you?"

"I don't know. It's very weird. And a little creepy, don't you think?" He was staring at the case as if he expected it to provide the answer.

"Maybe they stole it from you and wanted to return it."

"Why would someone steal a cigarette case?"

"Because you shouldn't have been smoking? I mean, it wasn't legal, was it?"

"It was the seventies. No one cared."

"Are you going to use it?"

"Oh no. I don't smoke regulars anymore. I only smoke hundreds. Sadly, they wouldn't fit."

I lowered my voice and said, "Maybe it was Grace. I mean, if you looked away for second."

Before he could answer, I was pushed up against the wall and Ricky was in my face saying, "What the fuck man?"

"Excuse me?" I said—or rather would have said if I had been able to take a breath.

Marc pulled him off me, saying, "Ricky, stop it. He didn't do anything to you."

"I told you I was okay with faggots. Didn't you hear me?"

"Oh my God! Ricky!" Marc said. "Did you say it that way? Did you really say you're okay with faggots?"

"Well, I am. And I meant it."

"Yeah, well, if you said, 'I'm okay with gay guys,' that sounds like you might be okay with gay guys," Marc explained. Much more patiently than I could have. "But when you say, 'I'm okay with faggots,' that does not sound like you're okay with gay guys!"

"Really?"

"Yes, really."

Ricky seemed to be thinking about that—something of a struggle—but then said, "That doesn't make what he wrote on my mirror okay."

"Someone..." I was having a little trouble catching my breath. "Someone... wrote... on your... mirror?"

"Don't even try! You're the only one who could have done it."

"But I was down at this end of the hallway serving drinks."

"And having a conversation with me," Marc added.

I tried to think: Could someone have slipped into or out of the Durante room while Marc and I were talking? Could we have not noticed? They'd have had to come into the hallway after Ricky went to the bathroom and then done whatever they did, and then gone back the way they came.

Finn could have done it. Or his manager. But I couldn't see why they would.

"What does it say?" I asked.

Ricky turned and walked down the hallway. We followed him. Standing in the doorway, we could see that someone had written a single word on the mirror in bronzer.

COCKSUCKER

Directly under the mirror was a pile of tissues that looked as though they'd been used to wipe the hands of the—writer? Scribbler? Graphiti-ist? Anyway, tissues were used to wipe the hands of whoever wrote that nasty word. Ricky stepped forward and grabbed a handful. Then he tried to wipe the offending word away, but ended up just making a big brown smear.

Meanwhile, I was trying to work it out. Whoever wrote that word must have known how much it would upset Ricky. But did they know that because they knew it was a word that would upset most straight guys when it got hurled at them? Or did they know it would specifically upset him because he'd partaken in the action at some point? I mean, teenage boys do all sorts of crazy things. Not that I... Well, I just wasn't *that* sort of teenage boy. I was barely that sort of grown-up boy.

Then we heard Wendy coming down the hall, calling out, "I'd like all actors on stage for a dance rehearsal."

Dance rehearsal? They were doing a dance? Marc hadn't mentioned dance. I looked at him. Obviously, he was as surprised as I was. But *where* could they be rehearsing this dance? Between the set for *Guessmate?* and the audience risers, there wasn't a lot of room to rehearse a dance. Not to mention, where would they shoot it once it was rehearsed? This was really weird. And given the things that had happened in the last ten minutes, that was saying something.

Marc looked down the hallway and called out, "Wendy, what *are* you talking about?"

"We're going to do a little dance number. Just like old times."

"You didn't warn us about this. I didn't bring dance clothes."

My guess was Marc didn't actually own dance clothes.

"There's nothing to worry about. It's two minutes, max. We'll intercut it with a number from the original show."

"So people can see how much we suck now?"

She laughed, and said, "You're always so funny, Marc!" She continued coming down the hallway toward us, calling for people to come rehearse. When she reached us, she looked at me and said, "Do you need something to do?"

"No, um, actually…" I pointed vaguely toward the spot where the table was on the other side of the wall, then said, "Excuse me." And I scurried out to the stage.

When I reached the table it was fully set up. The first 'wave' as Louis called it was nuts, M&Ms, Louis' loaded oatmeal cookies, carrots and celery with humus, corn chips and homemade guacamole, lavender shortbread, strawberries dipped in chocolate, and asparagus wrapped in ham. A lot, I know. But I wasn't surprised. It was, after all, Louis.

"Everyone's all set with drinks?" Louis asked.

"Weird things are happening."

"Oh? Do tell."

"Not good-weird things. Weird-weird things. When Marc was a teenager, he had a cigarette case."

"Yes, *that* surely made him a weird child."

"He lost it. Fifteen years ago. But tonight it was in the drawer of his makeup table."

"You're right. That is kinda weird-weird."

"And… someone wrote the word 'cocksucker' on Ricky's mirror. In bronzer."

"Also, weird-weird. But not an unpleasant thought, come to think of it."

I just shook my head. Out of the corner of my eye I noticed Eldridge smiling at me in the cutest way. I looked away. Donald and Ed had already set up a monitor and VCR on a stand they'd gotten from somewhere. There had to be some kind of equipment room on site with the basics. A video was paused. I wondered if that was why I'd heard music when I was in the craft room.

Now they were setting up a video camera with a microphone end onto a tripod. They'd brought that with them. It was professional grade. I know a little about video cameras since I once considered renting them out of the store. Honestly though, it would have been a huge expense for very little return.

Noticing that I'd been watching them set up, Louis said, "His name is Ed. Did you notice his forehead is peeling a little bit? I think we know where he was last Sunday."

"LA Pride isn't the only place the sun shines." I took a closer look then said, "And it doesn't look like it's peeling at all."

"A man can dream can't he?"

I decided to get this back on track. "Should we be worried about the weird stuff?"

"Someone doesn't like Ricky. Not a big surprise. Someone stole Marc's cigarette case and felt guilty about it for fifteen years," he said. Then he shrugged. "That's all."

He was probably right. I said, "Okay. Fine. What do you need us to do?"

"Not much really. One of us should be here at the table at all times. There's more of everything underneath, don't let anything run out. Every so often make sure people have drinks. We'll do breakfast about halfway through. And that's it. Did I hear Wendy talking about a dance rehearsal?"

"Yeah."

"I'd better go find Marc. He's not going to be happy about

dancing. I tried to teach him the two-step at Oil Can Harry's one time. He twisted an ankle and was out of work for a week."

He hurried off, leaving me with Eldridge who was still smiling at me. "I'm really glad we're getting to spend time together."

"Eldridge, we spend time together at the store."

"Not really. You're always hiding in your office."

"I'm not hiding... per se."

There was the D.W. Griffith Memorial Office; I wondered if I should go hide in there. It was tempting. I didn't though. I just looked around, trying to think of a reason to walk away.

In addition to a large desk that would seat five, the *Guess-mate?* set had three curtain-covered entrances: One for the team on the left, one for the team on the right, and one in the center for the host. Red-yellow-blue.

Donald—or more probably Ed—had found a stool and placed it in front of the red curtain. My guess was they'd be moving it around, so that when the show cut from one actor to another the backgrounds would change.

The actors were gathering: Grace, Keely, Meg and Ricky. Wendy scurried over to the monitor and put a video into the VCR. She immediately paused it.

"All right kids. I've picked out one of the numbers you did many, many times. I'm going to play it and then we'll try going through it slowly. Then we'll play it again and try to dance along. Where's Marc? Is he coming?"

"So, like, where are Finn and Kathleen?" Ricky asked.

"I sent them tapes earlier in the week. They've already rehearsed."

"What?" Grace said. "Why didn't we get tapes? We could have rehearsed too!"

"You'll be fine. Don't worry."

"That doesn't answer my question."

"Uh-huh," and with that she began the video. There was the teenaged cast of *Kapowie!* singing and dancing their hearts out.

The choreography looked simple enough, but not so simple a nondancer could quickly pick it up.

Out of the corner of my eye, I noticed Marc and Louis at the edge of the stage. Clearly, Marc did not want to do this. Louis hadn't been able to coax him all the way onto the stage. And then Donald was standing next to me, saying, "Helper number one."

He meant me.

"Noah," I reminded him.

"Sure, whatever. Can you come over and sit on the stool so we can make some decisions about lighting?" He posed it as a question, but it wasn't really. Well, I had been looking for a reason to walk away from the craft table.

Glancing over at Eldridge, I gave him a 'not my fault' shrug, then followed Donald over to the spot where they'd set up the camera. I got on the stool while he and Ed focused the camera on me. Meanwhile, across the room in front of the risers, Marc reluctantly joined the rehearsal. The video had played through once. Wendy was about to replay it so they could dance along.

"You know, Wendy, I haven't danced in fifteen years," Marc said. "I hope you're not expecting much. I'm certainly not."

"Me either," Meg said. "I haven't danced in ages."

"It's all right, Meg. You're going to be in the back."

"I know I'm in the back. I'm always in the back."

"Can I be in the back, too?" Marc asked.

"Oh, no... It's funny when you do it wrong."

"I don't necessarily agree with that," he said.

Wendy burst out laughing as though it had been a joke.

"Helper Number One, could you look to the left," Donald asked.

I didn't bother to tell him my name for a third time. Obviously, he had no interest in learning it. I looked to the left as instructed.

"My left," he corrected. That would be the right, but okay. I looked to the right. To Ed he said, "He's short. Much shorter than Finn. This angle works for the girls, but you're going to want to lift the camera four or five inches for Finn."

I thought he was being a little harsh but didn't say so. After studying me through the viewfinder for almost a minute, Donald said, "Yeah, we need to move the stool about five inches to the left," he said. "My left."

I hopped off the stool and Ed came over to move it. I wasn't certain why they didn't just move the camera but, okay... Once the stool was moved I got back on it. Donald and Ed took turns staring at me through the viewfinder.

"Okay, look at my hand over here," Donald said, holding his left hand out as far as he could. "Yeah, yeah, that's it. What do you think, Ed?"

Ed looked into the viewfinder again and then nodded wordlessly.

"Great. Well, I guess that means we're ready," Donald said. He walked over to his wife, who was watching the cast dance and began whispering in her ear.

"Couldn't we have twenty minutes," I heard her say.

More whispering.

"Okay, fine, whatever."

She aimed the remote control at the video player and ran the video backward. "Listen everyone. Donald is going to start recording each of you catching us up on what you've been doing and remembering the show fondly. Let's run through this once and then we'll circle back later for another rehearsal."

"Or two," Marc said.

"Or two. Now..." She pressed play, and said, "Five, six, seven, eight..."

They attempted the dance. It did not go well. They weren't in synch, at all. Arms and legs seemed to be moving in every direction at once.

"Ricky," Wendy called out. "Try to be more fluid. Think of yourself as water. Loosen up those tight muscles."

It was hard to see how Ricky was worse than the others.

Honestly, though, Marc really was the worst. He was jerking and twisting and thrusting without any regard to the original choreography—or even rhythm itself.

"Meg, stay in the back."

"How much further back can I get?"

And then, mercifully, the number ended and they stopped.

"All right, kids," Wendy said. "We'll give that another try later on. If you have a minute, try to remember the steps in your dressing room. Help each other if you can. Right now, Donald is going to start calling you, one by one."

Getting off the stool which was soon to be occupied by someone else, I went over to the craft table and joined Louis and Eldridge. Marc walked over, saying, "Not a word. Not a single word." Louis and I looked at each other and smirked.

Marc shoved an oatmeal cookie into his mouth. Then said, "Umis merasser."

"Yes, dear, I know," Louis said. "But you knew it would be a disaster before we came."

Marc swallowed. "I didn't know it would be a disaster with *dancing*."

"Don't focus on that. Focus on our savings account. Think about being able to buy down our interest rate when we find a house."

I didn't know what that meant, but it sounded like a good thing. Donald and Wendy were having a powwow near the camera. Marc filled a plate with cookies and walked over to join Keely and Grace, who were walking through the dance routine in front of the risers.

"Just seven more hours," Louis said dryly. It did sound like a very long time. Then he said, "So, Eldridge, what kinds of things do you like to do for fun?"

"I like to read, watch movies, try new things... go on dates." The last bit was clearly directed at me. "I don't have a lot of free time, though. I'm a full-time student."

"I know. Noah said. Women's Studies?"

"Only because they don't have a Gay Studies department. Yet. Not that I haven't turned a lot of my classes gay."

Louis gave him a curious look and said, "Oh, do tell."

"Well... like last quarter I took a film appreciation class. It was a broad survey class. The entire history of movies. I wrote a paper on the intersection between gay culture and early Hollywood."

"That sounds fascinating. Don't you think that's fascinating, Noah?"

"The professor didn't think so. He gave me a B-minus and accused me of perpetuating stereotypes. His view is that Hollywood was created by kindly straight White Protestant men. But that's not true at all. No one thought movies would amount to anything, so what you'd call the establishment stayed away from them for the first few decades. That led to opportunity for Jews, women, gays and lesbians, even African Americans—though that was mainly in Chicago during the silent period."

"That sucks," Louis said. "I guess you're done with film classes."

"Oh no, there are three other really good professors. All gay. I gave one of them my paper and he said that he would have given it an A-plus. He's already mentioned it to the head of the department."

"Feisty. I like smart, feisty men. Don't you, Noah?"

I wanted to kill him; or at least maim him. Luckily there was nothing but spoons and butter knives on the table. Then, out of nowhere, Wendy stood next to us holding the bag of cups from Juicy Juice.

"Louis, you're to use these for people's juice drinks. Finn is going first. He would like a Giant Green Monster. You've got the recipe book, don't you?"

"Picked it up with the blender and the fruit."

"Good. Don't let anyone see it. It's all *very* proprietary. Donald's gone to get Finn. So if you could have the drink ready. We want him to be holding it during the interview."

Wow, talk about product placement.

"Sure thing," Louis said, taking the bag and walking away. Wendy smiled at us, and said, "Have you been to Juicy Juice? I have coupons, so don't leave without one."

"Are they just in the valley?" Eldridge asked.

"Oh, basin-snobs," she said in a very dismissive tone, then began filling a plate with three shortbread, five chocolate-covered strawberries, a handful of M&Ms and three of Louis' loaded oatmeal cookies. I started to worry we might run out of those.

A panicked look came over Wendy's face. "I forgot to take my medicine. I always take it with a snack before bed, but I'm not going to bed, am I?"

With a nervous giggle, she scurried over to the risers, near the impromptu dance rehearsal.

"Oh yes, kids, that's much better."

She found her bag in the front row. Taking a bite out of an oatmeal cookie, she chewed as she dug through her purse—and dug through her purse, and then dug through her purse some more.

I reached under the table and brought up a few more cookies. Oh yeah, we were going to run out of those.

Meanwhile, Donald returned to the stage, without Finn. Looking up, Wendy saw him. Taking a cookie out of her mouth, she said, "Donald, I can't find my meds. I remember putting them in my bag."

"You must not have."

"You were right there, didn't you see?"

"I had other things on my mind."

"You had other things on your mind? More important things than your wife's health?"

"Wendy, are you going to die without it?"

"That isn't the point."

"I think it is."

She got up and went over to him to continue what was threatening to be a real blowout. I was trying to pay attention, without looking like I was paying attention, when Meg walked onto the stage. There was a big smile on her face.

Seeing us standing by the table, she said, "Can you believe I'm going first? And look... Keely got me a troll doll." She held up a naked, plastic troll doll with neon orange hair.

I glanced over at Keely who was saying, "Did I hear my name?"

Meg mouthed, "Thank you," and held up the doll.

Keely's brow wrinkled. It was obvious she had no idea what Meg was talking about. I looked back to Meg who seemed not to notice Keely's confusion. To whoever was nearby, she said, "I collected them when I was on the show. My makeup table was like a little village. Keely I'm so touched."

"Meg, I have no idea what you're talking about."

"Oh, you don't need to be shy."

But I was sure she wasn't being shy. I was sure she hadn't the slightest idea where the doll came from. Which meant the doll had appeared out of nowhere.

SEVEN

"What is Meg doing here?" Wendy asked Donald.

"Finn's not ready."

"Why didn't you get Kathleen?"

"And risk her finding out she was second choice?"

Meg looked a little less happy finding out she was second, well third choice. Donald said to her, "Don't be afraid, come on up."

Then Louis was there announcing, "One Giant Green Monster!"

"Oh God. No! No! No! That's for Finn. He's not ready yet. Put it on ice. It'll be fine for half an hour. We need a Mango Mania."

"Excuse me?" Louis said, trying to catch up.

"Now! We need a Mango Mania, now!"

Louis turned around and went back to the craft room. Wendy noticed the troll doll in Meg's hands, and said, "Did you bring that for Grace? She used to collect them."

"No. I'm the one who collected them."

"I don't think so. I'm sure it was Grace."

"It wasn't me," Grace said from her seat in the front row.

"It wasn't?" Wendy said. "Then who was it?"

"Me."

"No, it wasn't you. It couldn't have been Kathleen, could it?"

"Oh gosh, Wendy, it was *me*."

"Well. If you say so, dear."

A furious Louis returned, holding a hastily made Mango Mania. Meg was seated on the stool in front of the red curtain. I stood at the table with Eldridge. Ricky and Keely had come out to nibble, while Marc and Grace sat in the front row gossiping. Donald and Wendy were behind the camera taking turns looking into the viewfinder.

Louis said, "A-hem."

Wendy turned around. Seeing the drink, she said, "Oh wonderful."

Taking it, she said to Louis, "Now, did I explain you're the only one to make the drinks? No one else is to even look at the recipe book or the proprietary ingredients. Am I clear?"

"We've gone over this. Three times."

"Well. Good. Then you'll remember. It's important."

Louis turned and walked over to the table to stand with us while she brought the drink over to Meg, who immediately went to take a sip. Wendy nearly shrieked. "Hold on, Meg, let's get your first *honest* reaction. Ready Donald?"

He studied the camera carefully then pressed a button. "Action."

"Stop!" Wendy said, then she went over and adjusted the cup so that the Juicy Juice logo was more prominent. "Okay."

Frowning, Donald again said, "Action."

Meg took a long sip of her Mango Mania, smiling and saying, "Wow, that *is* good. Sweet."

Donald left a pause, then said in a smooth, fatherly voice, "So, Meg, tell us about who you are today."

After a moment, Meg nervously began, "Well, uh, after *Kapowie!* ended, I went to UCLA where I studied botany. I'm currently a professor at Cal State Fullerton, where I teach..."

"So, you're a science teacher?" Donald asked.

"A botanist."

"A science teacher."

"Well… I suppose you could say I'm a science teacher, yes. *Professor* is more accurate, though. I do have a doctorate."

"And is there a man in your life?"

Her brow wrinkled. "The dean, I suppose."

"You're dating the dean?"

"No. God, he's like ninety. Oh dear, could you not put that in? I really don't want to insult the dean. He's a nice man who's probably only seventy."

"So, you're single?"

"I'm far too busy to worry about men."

"Lonely, isn't it?"

"Not really."

"Cats?"

"What?"

"Do you have cats?"

"Just one."

"Oh, that's so sweet. What's your cat's name?"

"My cat's name is Agnes. After Agnes Arber who was a famous bot—"

"Do you call her Aggie?"

"No, I call her Agnes. Because that's what I named her."

"Getting back to men… Hold on, let's take a little break." He pressed the button to stop filming. "Meg, it's okay to talk about how lonely you are."

"But I'm not lonely. I just said I'm too busy to be lonely. And this show is for kids. Why would I talk about loneliness? Even if I was lonely. Which I'm not."

Donald shrugged and said, "OTN wants to promote womanly values. Let's give it another shot." He pressed the button. "Action."

Meg just looked at the camera a moment before she tried again, "Not to toot my own horn, but I recently published a paper in *The Annals of Botany* on the ways we might genetically modify plants to survive the effects of greenhouse gases. It was *very* well received."

Donald whispered loudly to Wendy, "Greenhouse gases? What is she talking about? This is going to be really hard to edit."

"Cut," Wendy said. "Listen, Meg, the science stuff isn't going to fly. Could you talk about when you used to do the home-making and cooking sections of the show and how helpful they are now that you're a grown-up woman. And maybe how you're hoping to cook your way into a man's heart."

"I don't cook."

"That has nothing to do with this. If you could just... take another stab at who you are now. Science teacher. Lonely spinster with cats."

"One cat."

"It's fine to exaggerate."

"But—"

Wendy stepped in close to say a few more things to Meg. I looked at the others gathered around the table. Ricky and Keely were each holding plates and nibbling.

Keely swallowed, then said, "They were like this when we were on the show. Always forcing us into stereotypes. Creating narratives that had nothing to do with who we actually were."

"They're going to love me," Ricky said. "They always made me play the nerd on the show and now I'm a jock. That's an arc. Arcs are great for TV. They're gonna eat it up."

"They always made me play the Black girl who doesn't act like a Black girl. I doubt they want anything else from me."

I glanced at Eldridge who was giving me your basic, 'Where *are* we?' look.

"Okay," Wendy said, loudly. "We're ready to give this another try. Meg, take another sip and center yourself. Whenever you're ready."

She nodded at Donald who said, "Action."

After a beat, Meg said, "Hi! It's me, Meg."

"Tell us, Meggie, what have you been up to?" Donald asked.

"Well, after the show I went to college and now I'm a science teacher. Still looking for the right guy... maybe someday. Still practicing my upside-down pineapple cake hoping to catch a man. My favorite thing about teaching is the kids. I hope to have a bunch of my own someday. When I meet that right guy. In the meantime, I have the most adorable kitty to keep me company. Her name's Aggie. I'm thinking about getting another one. You know, to keep Aggie company. Sometimes she gets lonely. I mean, we all do. Right?"

"What do you miss most about *Kapowie!*" Donald asked.

"Oh gosh. So much. I think I miss my castmates. They still mean so much to me. Getting to sing and dance with them. Tell jokes. Being kids together. Oh gosh, it's so wonderful to think about."

After a pause, Wendy said, "Oh that was wonderful, Meg! Such a good job."

Meg smiled weakly at the praise, before asking, "Is that all you need?"

"It is for now," Donald said. "Hopefully there will be time at the end, and we'll be able to do some additional shots. So if you think of anything you'd like to add—"

"I won't. Do you think I could go home now?"

"Oh no, no, no..." Donald said.

"We need you for the dance number," Wendy said.

"Even though I'm in the back where no one will see me?"

"Yes, even though you're in the back."

Meg walked over to where Marc and Grace were sitting in the front row of the risers. They watched her sympathetically. Well, Grace did. Marc was looking at Donald in a way I could only describe as dangerous. Kind of like a lion cornered. I thought he might hiss.

Looking around, Donald called out, "Ricky! My man! How about you go next?"

"Sure thing."

"Great. We'll go in a couple of minutes. Is that the shirt you want to wear?"

"Is it okay?"

"Do you have something with sleeves?"

"Yeah, all right."

As he left, Donald and Wendy came over to the craft table.

"Oh, this all looks just great," Donald said, immediately picking up a chip and scooping up about half a cup of guacamole.

"Yes, this is all wonderful. Thank you, Louis. What are the little specks in the shortbread?"

"Lavender."

"Oh my," Wendy said, setting a piece back down.

"Keely," Donald said. "You don't have a lighter shade of foundation?"

"I'm not wearing foundation."

"It's just with the backdrops we're using... We'd like you to pop."

For a moment, it seemed like she might say something. Instead, she walked over and joined the three others in the audience. Surprised, Donald asked his wife, "Was that a yes?"

Wendy was stacking strawberries onto a plate. "Donald, I think this time we need to show the actors the clips from the show we're considering. Help them get back into character."

Donald shrugged. "They should be more professional than that."

"Well... they're not." She took a folded-up sheet of paper out of her pocket while saying, "Louis, we're going to need a..." She found what she wanted on the sheet. "... a Pineapple Punch for Ricky."

He took a step away, but I said, "Actually, Wendy, Ricky said he wanted a Banana Blast." I was beginning to think I might be good at this craft table thing.

She studied me for a long moment, as though I was something unpleasant left on her doorstep. Then she said, "A fan.

Well, I suppose that makes this easy. Louis, we need a Banana Blast!"

As Louis walked away, she shoved a very large strawberry into her mouth. Chewing, she said, "Also... Donald, this time let's try to break things up. Talk about the juice first, how much he likes—"

Ricky was back, wearing a black polo that was at least two sizes too small. He said, "I get to talk about my gyms."

"Sure. Tit for tat," Wendy said before turning back to her husband. "Just let them say whatever they want about themselves. If it doesn't work, we'll reshape it and ask them to try again. Then go on to some reminiscence about how fondly they remember the show. The whole show's only going to be a half an hour. We need roughly a minute with each cast member, more for Finn and Kathleen. We'll interview ourselves, and the rest will be highlights from the series."

By the end of her instructions Donald was clearly seething. Obviously, he was the kind of guy who relied on his wife to tell him what to do. He was also the kind of guy who didn't see himself that way and hated her for helping. He said, "Got it" so sharply that I was surprised he didn't draw blood.

"My gyms need to make the final cut," Ricky said, having picked up on at least some of what they'd been saying. "I want a verbal agreement on that. In front of witnesses." He waved a hand at me and Eldridge.

"Mmmm-hmmm. Don't worry about it," Donald said, which wasn't exactly agreement.

Ricky took his place on the stool. Donald and Ed spent quite a bit of time looking into the viewfinder and making adjustments, while Wendy ate strawberries. A tiny bit later, Louis delivered the Banana Blast to Ricky and came over to the table.

"Are there more oatmeal cookies?" Eldridge asked. "We're almost out."

"Yeah, in one of the... Oh! How about you go grab them out of one of the bags?"

"Sure," Eldridge said, before walking off.

I stared at Louis. He'd clearly wanted to get rid of him. As Ricky began his bit, I leaned over and whispered to Louis, "That wasn't very subtle."

He shrugged then whispered back, "How are the nightmares?"

Also, not subtle. I almost said he didn't know what he was talking about, but it was June in Los Angeles and far too warm to close bedroom windows. Marc and Louis slept directly below me. Or, at least tried to, as I apparently let out the occasional yelp.

"I think they're getting better. I hope they are. Maybe I should be asking you."

"The first few times it happened Marc thought you were having sex. I pointed out it didn't sound like happy sex."

"And you think I'm a happy sex kind of guy?"

"Totally." After a moment, he said, "If you need to talk about it, I'm here for you."

I said, "Thanks," but knew I wouldn't be talking to him about it. I mean, I had talked to him about it. After I'd been kidnapped and nearly murdered, I told my friends everything that had happened. I took it all in stride. *We* took it all in stride.

Honestly, even as it was happening, I took it in stride. I mean, people threaten your life enough times and it becomes kind of normal, right? But... the weird thing was that the dreams weren't about being kidnapped, or finding one of my employees dead, or having a gun waved in my face, or waking up with a dead person, or finding a corpse in my garbage bin... In fact, they weren't really about anything. The dreams were little more than a feeling. I knew I was in bed. I knew I was alone. But I'd be feeling fear, fear that wasn't like anything I'd ever felt. Worse than what I'd felt in any of the actual situations I just mentioned. Irrational fear. Growing fear. Fear that made me yelp—well, scream. A little.

And then Eldridge was back with a giant plastic bag full of cookies, and Ricky was in front of the camera saying, "So, yeah, I've got three gyms: one in Studio City, one in Van Nuys, one in

Sherman Oaks. I mean, when I was on the show, I was this skinny, brainy little nerd. And I want everyone to know that you don't have to stay that way. You don't gotta be skinny or brainy or a nerd forever. You *can* turn your life around. Just come to a Lift for Life gym and we'll make you one hundred percent muscle."

"Did he just do a commercial?" I whispered to Louis.

"Sure did."

Wendy heard us and turned around putting a finger over her lips to shush us.

Donald asked, "What's your favorite memory of being on *Kapowie!*"

"The friendships. I've been friends with these people nearly twenty years. I mean... Finn, what a great guy. Kathleen is always there if you need a kind, comforting word. Little Marc—well, not so little anymore—always there with a joke. Hey Marc, if you're listening, come by one of my gyms and I'll give you a free membership."

I glanced back at Marc who looked like he might explode. Clearly, he was not enjoying any of this.

"Keely, you're my sista, girl. And Meg, don't worry, there's a man out there for you."

There was a pause, during which Grace stage whispered, "He forgot about me, thank God."

"What about Wes?" Donald asked.

"Oh man, I wish I knew where he was. I miss that dude. Miss him a whole lot." He appeared to be choking up. He looked away, as though struggling to keep his composure.

After a slight pause, Donald said, "And... cut. That was great, just great, Ricky. Exactly what we're looking for."

"Great, thanks, guys. I appreciate it," he said with a big sunny smile.

And then, rather foolishly as it turned out, Donald said, "Marc, would you like to go next?"

EIGHT

"I'm glad we're just craft services," Eldridge said as Marc walked away. "I don't think there's a single thing I could say about myself that Donald would be okay with."

"Did you ever see the show?"

It had been for kids younger than I was but only by a few years. He was probably—

"Oh yeah, I watched it all the time when I was like... eight, maybe? It was syndicated to one of the independent stations."

I would have been just going off to college. Though why that mattered, I couldn't have said. "What did you think of it?"

"I liked it. I actually had kind of a crush on Marc."

"Really? I thought people had crushes on Finn or Wes."

"Oh yeah, they were cute. But I've always had different tastes."

Honestly, I wasn't sure how to take that. He wanted to go out with *me*. Was I part of 'different tastes'? Did I *want* to be part of different tastes?

Marc was making himself comfortable on the stool, as Wendy called out, "Louis! Could you make Marc an O.J. Sumptuous." Immediately, she added to anyone standing nearby, "We're probably going to be changing that name."

"Actually, Wendy, I'm not thirsty," Marc said.

The look on her face was like a window shutting. "You can just hold the cup, that's okay."

"I'm not selling your drinks for you. You're not paying me for that."

"Marc, you're not a celebrity. There's no reason to pay you for holding a cup. Plus, I'm trying to give you a free drink. They're four ninety-five in our store. Some people have one every day."

That made me wonder if they were paying Finn Henderson to hold the cup. Is that where all the money went? Were they paying Kathleen too? Or, more likely, making a donation to her church so she wouldn't have to pay taxes on it.

"You're right, I'm not a celebrity," Marc said. "So it shouldn't matter that I don't want to hold your slushie, should it?"

"It's not a—What do you want?" Wendy asked, her voice as hard and bitter as a stone.

"I want to be able to talk about myself. I'm gay, in case you hadn't figured that out. I want to talk about my partner, Louis. I want to say that we're very, very happy. Because we are."

"Yeah, but this is a show for kids," Donald said.

"I was a kid once. All gay people start out as kids. You do know that, don't you? We don't just show up out of nowhere, fully grown and ready to go clubbing. Do you have any idea what it would mean to all the gay kids who saw this if I talked about who I am and the simple fact of being happy in a relationship with another man?"

Louis applauded. Eldridge joined him. I felt I had to start applauding too. I mean, I wanted to—and also, they'd probably kill me if I didn't. Grace was applauding, so were Meg and Keely. It was turning into a Spartacus moment. Ricky was pointedly not applauding, nor was Ed—which did suggest Louis was wrong about the whole sunburn thing. Of course, Donald and Wendy did not applaud. In fact, they were looking pretty angry. Or angrier.

"All right, all right," Donald said. "Look, you're absolutely right. You should get to say whatever you want about yourself. You all should. The problem is, OTN is not going to put that on the air. And so I'd have to edit it. If you say nothing they'll allow, I'll have nothing to work with."

"Why is this such a problem? There was a gay guy on *The Real World* two years ago," Marc said. He and Louis had actually gotten cable installed just so they could watch.

"Yeah, that's MTV," Donald said. "This is OTN owned by BTN."

"What's OTN?" Meg asked.

"Old Time Network," I said.

"And BTN?"

"Believe Television Network."

BTN also had a line of videos I didn't stock, but I had seen them in the trade publications. I couldn't believe I hadn't realized this before. I was pretty sure BTN was the network Kathleen and her husband were on. Which, now that I was thinking about it, must be the reason she was there. And, now that I was thinking about it some more, it would also be the whole reason OTN bought the broadcast rights to *Kapowie!* in the first place. Because Kathleen was on it. She was the big star there, not Finn.

Speaking of Finn, he was suddenly standing there with Amber. He was still wearing his sunglasses. In one hand he held the Juicy Juice with his name on it. Looking down, he said in a deep, gravelly, knee-weakening voice, "I'm ready, Donald. Let's do this."

"Louis!" Wendy nearly screamed. "Could you get Mr. Henderson his Giant Green Monster."

"We already got it," Amber said. "It was in the craft room. His name was on it."

"Yeah, but... I, like, finished it. May I have another?" He sounded a bit like a well-behaved little boy.

"Of course, you can have another," Wendy said. "I'm so glad you liked it."

Louis left the stage to go make the drink. Donald hurried over to lead Finn over to the stool, practically pushing us out of the way—well, not practically, actually pushing us out of the way. I nearly fell down.

As they got close to the stool, Amber said, "No, no… that's not going to work. We need to use the blue curtain. Finn is never shot in front of anything red, orange or brown. It's simply wrong for his coloring."

Ed quickly moved the camera and tripod approximately fifty feet so that it sat in front of the sparkly blue curtain on the other side of the stage. Donald followed with the stool. Finn and Amber stayed where they were while Donald and Ed re-focused the camera.

Marc said, "I need a cigarette."

Nearby, Grace said, "Me too."

Ricky and Keely had taken seats in the front of row of the audience section—not together; several seats apart. They looked completely uninterested in each other. She was definitely not his 'sista'.

Meg had come over to the table with Eldridge and me. On the surface, at least, I was checking the table to see what might need refilling. Really though, I was deciding if I wanted a snack. Lowly Helper One was entitled to eat.

I took an asparagus spear wrapped in ham and was trying to casually slip it into my mouth, when Eldridge edged next to me and said, "It seems like all the drama is happening off-screen. Is that normal?"

I withdrew the asparagus spear, and said, "I don't know. I mean, I met my ex on a set. He was a production designer and I was a PA. I ran a lot of errands, so I wasn't actually on set much. That was the only time I ever actually… Anyway, later on he used to come home and talk about the crazy things that happened, so maybe it *is* normal."

I bit off half the spear and started chewing before he could ask me another question.

"It's normal for *this* show," Meg said. "It was nothing but drama the whole time we were shooting."

On the *Guessmate?* set, Finn was now seated on the stool, and they'd begun the process of aiming the camera to frame Finn the way he wanted to be framed. Amber demanded to look through the viewfinder every minute or so. Then she'd stand back and bark directions. "Higher, lower, left, right."

Louis was back with the new Giant Green Monster. He handed it to Finn, who immediately drank about a quarter of the drink. I noticed Wendy was tempted to jump in and tell him to wait, as she had with Meg, but she stopped herself. People like Finn got to do whatever they wanted.

Donald was standing close to Finn talking very quietly, as though he didn't want the rest of us to hear, as though somehow Finn's portion of the show would be different from everyone else's. *Well, it probably would be,* I thought. It was very likely Donald would let him talk about his trouble with drugs and his time in rehab. It would be considered a good warning for kids. If Marc had gone to rehab for being gay, then Donald would probably agree to let him talk about it.

As Donald whispered, Finn continued drinking his drink. Louis was still nearby, so I stepped over and asked, "What's in that drink? He seems to really like it."

"Bananas and peaches, coconut milk, frozen yogurt, a secret powder, and green goop that looked like spinach, kale, collard green—and possibly some yard clippings. Probably mostly frozen spinach, though."

"That sounds disgusting."

"I couldn't bring myself to try it," Louis said. "The secret powder is 'proprietary'. She made a point of telling me not to even try to figure out what's in it."

"Yeah? So, what's in it?"

"As nearly as I can tell, protein powder made of whey—the kind body builders use, possibly some cheap powdered baby formula and a lot of confectionary sugar. And I mean a lot."

"So, basically, they're selling fruit flavored icing and calling it a healthy drink?"

"Pretty much, yeah."

"No wonder people love it."

Finn obviously loved it. He kept taking long sips. Donald stepped away and Finn took off his sunglasses. His eyes were a shocking pale blue. Under the lights, his pupils constricted so there was even more of that remarkable color. They were his most unique feature, and it was ironic that he wore sunglasses so often to cover them.

"Are you ready, Finn?"

"Can I get another one of these?" he said, sipping the last of his drink. Three? He was going to drink three of those disgusting drinks? Wendy looked across the stage at Louis and raised her eyebrows in command—causing her to look a bit like her husband. Louis got the message and hurried off.

Now Amber was intently whispering to Finn. I began to wonder: This was a where-are-they-now episode of a show that no longer existed. What could possibly be so important it needed to be whispered about? And for so long? By more than one person?

Marc and Grace were back, and Marc was saying, "Something's weird. The door won't open."

"The door to your dressing room?"

"No, the outside door. The exit door. We went to have a cigarette and it wouldn't open."

"Well, that's weird. That door has a panic bar." After the quake, I had to have one installed on the backdoor of the store. The front door already had one. I turned to Eldridge, and said, "Maybe you should stay here. I'm going to go look at this door."

Marc, Grace and I walked back to the door we'd come through less than two hours before. I walked up to it and pushed the panic bar. It behaved normally; it moved when I pushed it, but the door didn't open. In fact, it didn't budge. I pushed on the panic bar a couple more times.

"It's supposed to open."

"Do you think someone locked it from the outside?" Marc asked.

"You can't do that," I said. If you lock it from the outside, it prevents people from getting in but anyone inside can still get out. That's the whole point of the door, that no one gets locked in."

"Why can't we open it, then?" Grace asked.

"There must be something stuck between the door and the doorjamb. Maybe a shim or something."

I only knew what a shim was because the house Jeffer and I owned was built in the twenties and at one point we had to hire a carpenter to rehang a couple of doors that were threatening to never close again. He had to take off the molding and slip in some shims. An expensive education in carpentry.

"Why would someone do that?" Marc asked.

"Duh, they don't want us to get out," Grace said.

"There must be other doors," I said. "Only having one exit wouldn't be up to code. One of the other doors has to be open."

We turned around and walked down the hallway, passed the dressing rooms. There was another exit just beyond the D.W. Griffith Memorial Office where I'd found the pen I didn't have to use. I quickly walked up to that door and pushed its panic bar. The door didn't open. It was also jammed shut.

Without any discussion, we turned and headed across the stage to the far corner. We walked behind the set to the third exit door. I pushed, no longer expecting much, and was absolutely right. It wouldn't open.

"Something's really wrong," I said. Then we walked behind the *Guessmate?* set to the final corner. I hurried over to that last door and pushed the bar. Once again, nothing happened. Nothing at all.

Sweat broke out on my forehead, I turned to Marc and Grace, and said, "We're trapped."

NINE

"That's so typical," Grace said.

"The producers locked you in when you were kids?" I asked, somewhat horrified.

"Not that I remember," she said. "But they did flagrantly disregard our health and safety."

"*Flagrantly*," Marc repeated. "We should go talk to Donald. Give him an earful."

Feeling edgy, I closed my eyes and tried to imagine myself in a bright sunny meadow rather than trapped in a sound stage. I added flowers to the meadow. Yellow. Red. Purple. Too many flowers. I subtracted some. There was a nice breeze, cool, comforting—

"What are you doing?" Marc asked.

"Trying not to panic."

"We're trapped in here. Panic is appropriate."

I didn't find that helpful at all. Marc grabbed me and pulled me around the set until we stepped through the red curtain, which put us on the opposite side of the set from where Finn was being filmed. Amber noticed us first, and yelled, "Cut! Cut! Cut! Get them out of Finn's eyeline."

Donald spun around and said, "What are you doing? You

can't just walk through the curtains! Not while we're taping! Did everyone hear that? NO ONE WALK THROUGH THE CURTAINS!"

"Donald…" Marc started forcefully. "We need to talk."

"Now is not the time to talk about your radical liberal agenda. Finn is taping."

"Donald," Grace said, behind me. "The doors are jammed."

His manner changed completely. He turned around and said, "Finn, buddy, we're going to take the tiniest little break."

Finn was barely paying attention. He'd put his glasses back on and was staring up at the studio lights as though they were constellations. "It's cool."

And then Donald came over to us, sweeping us off the *Guessmate?* set and into a corner of the soundstage near the entrance.

"Now, quietly tell me what this is about," he said, as though we'd been the ones yelling.

Marc said, "We wanted to go have a cigarette, but all the doors are jammed shut. What's going on?"

"Well, for one thing… you really shouldn't be smoking."

"So I've heard. Still, I'd like to go outside and have a cigarette. Why are the doors jammed shut?"

"You can't just lock us in here, Donald," Grace said. "I'm sure that's against union rules. This is an AFTRA shoot, isn't it?"

"Let's be reasonable. The two of you need to calm down. Everything is under control."

"What do you mean everything's under control? We can't get out of the building!"

Grace said, "You didn't answer my question, Donald."

"We're doing everything according to AFTRA rules."

I sincerely doubted that but kept my mouth shut. Grace, on the other hand, said, "Locking us in here can't be according to the rules."

"We are absolutely following the rules. In spirit."

Then I realized Donald didn't seem surprised by the revelation at all. I said, "You knew about the doors, didn't you? There's a reason we're trapped in here. What is it?"

"All right, Helper Number One, this isn't really—"

"NOAH! My name is NOAH!"

I very nearly apologized for yelling, but was distracted when I realized my hands were shaking. I jammed them into my pockets. I'd managed to get the attention of everyone in the soundstage. I flushed.

Wendy came over, and asked, "What's happening?"

"I have everything under control, dear."

"It doesn't sound that way, Donald."

And then he said nothing for a long moment. A very angry long moment. His eyes flitted from one of us to another. Thinking. At least it looked like he was thinking. If he was thinking he was probably trying think up a lie.

When that didn't work, he leaned forward and quietly said, "You can't tell anyone. OTN didn't give us enough money to rent the studio *and* pay you."

"Donald—" Wendy said.

"No, I think the truth is better. You probably don't remember him, but the security guard who let us in? That's Alan, who was our stunt coordinator in the second season."

"You had a *stunt* coordinator?" I asked Marc.

"You don't want to know."

"Anyway, no one's supposed to know we're shooting in here. That's why we came in the way we did, while the guard at the north gate was on his break and wouldn't see us. That's why I had Alan shut us in. We can't have people wandering around the lot. If the other guard gets wind of us being here..."

"You'll have to pay him off too," Marc guessed.

"Exactly, and then how do we pay you?"

Something told me Donald and Wendy were getting paid before the actors. If there was a problem they wouldn't be taking any shortages out of their own pockets.

Wendy decided to do damage control. "That's not true.

Donald, you're making them think we don't have *any* money. The budget is fine. We have more than enough money to make the show. Everything will be fine."

"What if there's a fire?" I asked.

"Well, that doesn't have anything to do with the budget," Wendy said.

"What if there's a fire and we're locked in here?" I repeated.

"Then we pull the fire alarm and Alan will come," Donald said. "Plus, you know... sprinklers."

I looked up at the ceiling. I saw lights, metal girders from which the lights hung, electrical cords, cobwebs, mysterious dark nooks and crannies, a couple of catwalks—but no sprinklers. The building probably pre-dated that particular code. Right? Though, I suspected their insurance was high, it probably cost less than actually installing sprinklers. Nothing about this felt particularly safe.

"What about the elephant door?" Marc asked. "Can we open that? I promise not to go more than two feet from the stage."

The elephant door was on the west side of the building, near the entrance we used. It was a twenty-foot door and slid to one side to allow furniture and props (and occasionally elephants) to be loaded onto the stage.

Donald said, "I promised we wouldn't, for one thing... And for another, it does make a lot of noise. So, please don't go near it." He chewed his cheek for a moment. "You can smoke in the men's room."

"Donald, I'm not sure—"

"We have to let them smoke somewhere... dear."

"Thank you," Marc said.

He was about to storm off, when I asked Donald what seemed like an important question, "Isn't it your job to get enough money to make the production?"

Marc watched, waiting for the answer.

"We have enough money. I said that already," Wendy repeated.

"Where did you come from?" Donald wanted to know. "And what are *your* qualifications?"

"Noah owns Pinx Video," Marc said. "So he knows how to do things on the cheap."

"Wait a minute. I run a profitable business."

"That's what I meant."

"Look, I haven't worked in the industry in a long time, and I miss it. I really miss it," Donald said, nearly whining. "I may have over-promised. Just bear with me. I'm not supposed to talk about this, but I'm in negotiations with OTN to bring the show back. Isn't that exciting?"

"Donald, you're oversharing."

"None of that has anything to do with us," Grace said. "You'll be casting teenagers. Not us."

"There could be cameos," Donald said. "In fact, I could make sure there are cameos."

"Oh my Lord," his wife said.

"More opportunities to work all night for scale?" Grace asked. "I don't think so." To Marc she said, "Come on, let's go have a cigarette in the men's room like high school kids."

Louis was standing there with another Giant Green Monster. "What's going on?"

"We're locked in," Marc said.

"Is that some kind of industry lingo?"

"No, darling, they've jammed the doors so we can't go outside," Marc said.

"What?! Why?"

"Could you bring that over here," Amber called out to Louis. Meanwhile, Meg and Keely came over.

"Did you just say we can't get out of here?" Keely asked.

"Oh my gosh, I'm claustrophobic," Meg said.

Wendy heard her, and called out, "Oh for God's sake. It's a six thousand square foot building with a thirty-five-foot ceiling. You can't get claustrophobic." I had to be on Meg's side, though.

I was a little anxious thinking about how we couldn't—okay, a lot anxious.

Louis came back from giving Amber the drink for Finn. It didn't seem like either of them cared that we were trapped. Finn was happily pulling at his straw.

"Explain this to me," Louis said. So, I started to. Partway through, Marc said, "I'm dying for a cigarette. I'll be in the men's room with Grace."

The two of them scurried off.

Louis recapped, "So, we're not supposed to be here, which is why we can't go outside. They paid the guard but not the owners of the studio. They're doing this on a shoestring—oh crap. I only got a twenty-five percent deposit from them. If they don't pay me this will actually cost me money."

"Do you really think we won't get paid?" Keely asked. "I could really use the money. Flowers are a low margin business."

I tried to calm myself down. Breathing slowly. Honestly, I felt like running around the stage screaming 'We're trapped! We're trapped!' but maybe that wasn't reasonable. Maybe Donald was telling the truth, and it really wasn't a big deal. I walked back to the craft table telling myself again and again, "Not a big deal. Not a big deal."

Donald asked Finn if he was ready, and they began. Pressing the button on the camera, he said, "Action." Followed a few moments later with, "So, Finn, tell us what happened to you right after *Kapowie!* ended."

"Well, I was cast in *Young Leonardo* actually before *Kapowie!* ended."

Young Leonardo was a TV show that ran four seasons. I have the tapes at the store. In case you don't go in for television shows, it's the one about Leonardo DaVinci as a young artists' apprentice, solving mysteries and chasing women. On a slow day, he might dabble in painting and having genius ideas, but mostly he chased after girls and beat up bad guys because... that's what gay Renaissance artists did?

"We began filming almost the day after *Kapowie!* ended. I barely had time to throw a party between the shows." He smiled as though to acknowledge his reputation as a party boy.

The interesting thing about watching him was that as soon as the camera came on, he seemed to brighten. He was suddenly more alert, more charismatic, better looking, shinier. It was kind of weird, actually.

"The show was crazy popular," he continued. "People really responded to my performance. It meant a lot to a lot of people. And then I started making movies and didn't stop for almost ten years."

"More than half a billion dollars in box office," Donald said, obviously impressed. "Tell us, Finn, what's your favorite memory of *Kapowie!*?"

"Everything. The whole thing felt special. You know, it was all in front of us. The future. Even if we didn't make it, we knew we'd do something. It was like Christmas morning, and you've got these presents in front of you. You don't know what they are, you don't even know if you want them, but you know, you just know they're going to be great."

"That's really profound," Donald said.

"Thank you," Finn replied as though it actually was. He resumed sipping his drink.

Suddenly, everyone around me gasped. I turned to see that Kathleen was standing there with Gameboy-playing Heston. With her wig and her four-inch heels she was an Amazon towering over most of the people in the room. Certainly, she was much taller than her son. And me. Her dress was sprinkled with sparkles and her makeup was thick and carefully drawn. She didn't look like a woman, she looked like a creature from another dimension.

She and Finn saw each other. I thought for sure one of them, or maybe even both, would spontaneously combust. Looking back and forth I couldn't tell what they were feeling. It could have been anger, rage, love, lust, disgust, longing, passion, hatred.

Any one of those, all of those things—or, given that she was an evangelist and he was an actor, it could have been none of those things. It could have all been completely fake.

It got so quiet that even Heston looked up from his game. Then I noticed something I should have seen before. His eyes. They were the same exact blue as Finn's. Mentally, I subtracted the flat black hair obscuring the boy's face and there were Finn's cheekbones, his jaw, his chin. It was glaringly obvious that Finn was Heston True's real father.

TEN

And then, Kathleen spun on her very tall heels and left the stage. Her son trailed after her. We all gave each other 'what was that?' and 'oh my God' looks, but no one said a word for at least a minute.

Wendy stepped over and whispered something to Donald, who then he said, "Okay, uh, Finn, would you mind terribly saying something about Juicy Juice?"

"Sure, yeah, no problem."

Wendy rushed over to the stool and handed Finn a slip of paper. He read it quickly and then said, "Okay, we can go."

"Hey man, I want to thank you for this amazing juice drink from Juicy Juice right here in the valley. It's a delicious, healthy drink. I mean, this is my third. Right?"

Donald nodded over the camera. "Wonderful. Thank you." Then he asked, "Finn, what's the funniest thing you remember from the show?"

"The funniest thing? Wow, there's so much. I mean, man, we had fun, didn't we?" He stopped and thought for a moment. Like any good actor there seemed to be a lot going on behind his eyes. But was there? Was he thinking hard? Or was he just waiting to make his response as dramatic as possible. Then he said, "Wes. Wes and I playing pranks. Mostly on you, Donald. You used to drink a lot of coffee and we'd put vodka in it when you weren't looking. And then you wouldn't notice, which cracked us up."

"I, uh, I don't remember that."

"Well, yeah, you probably wouldn't. Another time we wrote our own filthy lyrics for one of the songs."

"Okay, that I remember."

There was a bit of a pause, and then Finn said, "I hope you don't mind, but there are a few things I'd like to say. I was taking drugs during that time. Not heroin. Not yet. Mostly coke. I mean, we didn't even think it was addictive back then. So, yeah, I was doing coke. And I had a doctor who would give me as much valium as I wanted, so I was always see-sawing between the two. The doctor eventually cut me off, and that's when I started doing heroin, snorting it at first, then smoking it, and eventually shooting up. By the time I started making movies, when *Young Leonardo* was on hiatus, I was a full-blown addict. I managed to be kind of sober when I was making films, but I did cause problems. Delays. I know I hurt people and I'm sorry for that. It's taken three stints in rehab to get me this far. I don't want to go backward. I won't go backward."

"We're all proud of you Finn. You've come a long way."

"Thank you." Then he said, out of nowhere really, "I feel sleepy."

"We're almost done," Donald said. "Remember to leave a beat for the edit, please." I could see him counting to five. Then, "Can you tell us about your new movie, *Running Toward Justice*?"

"It's about a drug deal gone wrong... an' no... is not auto... auto... is not about me. I'm serio-th, I'm gonna fall athleep." Then he laughed, and said, "My tongue feelth funny."

Amber yelled, "Cut!" Though I didn't remember anyone giving her permission to say that. She rushed over to Finn. With two fingers she opened one of his eyes. Then said, "You idiot."

"Wha... I didn'th do anythin. I'm jus tired. It's late. Isn't it late?"

Amber turned around, pointed at me and Eldridge, and said, "You two. Help me get him back to his dressing room." To Donald she said, "Give me an hour or two. I'll get him sobered up."

"I'm not high. Honeth." He began laughing at how foolish he sounded. "I have a lipth... Call the tabloids... Finn Henderson hath a lipth."

Eldridge and I got there to help him off the stool. We got on either side of him. My first thought was to let him get off the stool on his own, especially when he said, "I can do ith."

But when he tried he nearly fell, so Eldridge and I each took an arm and began to lead him off the *Guessmate?* set. As we led him around the giant desk, he said, "I don't feel too good."

Which, in my limited experience of alcohol and/or drugs, meant he was likely to puke.

"Let's take him that way," I said, nodding my head toward the southwest corner of the building. Since I'd quickly learned my way around while trying to find an open door, I knew that was the fastest way to get to Finn's dressing room.

We hurried him by the office, and then Amber was holding open the door to the Emery dressing room for us to enter. He immediately pushed away from us, rushed into the bathroom, and vomited. Loudly. Disgustingly. And presumably, very greenly.

"There's 7-Up and I'll look around to see if there's anything like a cracker," I said, trying to be helpful.

"Don't worry. I'll take of care of it. You don't need to do anything," she said that so confidently, I knew she'd done this before.

"Are you sure you can handle this? He doesn't need to go to the hospital—"

"No! God no! If he goes to the hospital, he'll never work again. You have no idea how hard it was to get him insured—"

There was another loud, gagging groan from the bathroom.

"Someone should be in there with him," Eldridge said.

"God damn it," Amber said, and then went into the bathroom, slamming the door behind her. That left Eldridge and I alone in the dressing room.

Eldridge mouthed the words, "Oh my God!"

I whispered, "Let's get out of here."

In the hallway, I said, "I think I should bring them some 7-Up anyway and just leave it. In case."

"He might need coffee. I mean, if he overdosed. *Is* he overdosing? What do you think he's on? He just said his problem is with heroin, right?"

"Amber said something about a speedball," I said.

"That's what killed John Belushi," Eldridge said.

"Wow, I'm impressed. You were barely even born when he died."

"I was seven or eight," Eldridge said as though that was somehow ancient. Or, at least, old enough to read tabloids.

We reached the craft room and found Louis and Marc in there. The light above them was still flickering. When he saw us, Louis said, "I can't believe this. I have to make a Jungle Juice... for Keely."

"You're kidding. And she's letting them?"

"She says she just wants to get this over with," Marc said.

I couldn't blame her there.

"What's going on with Finn?" Louis asked.

"Apparently, he's taken something," I said. "He's puking, but his manager says he'll be okay."

"Do you think he needs a doctor?"

"His manager is adamant that a hospital trip would ruin his career."

"Dying would also ruin his career."

"When did he find the time to take something?" Marc asked. "His manager has been with him the whole time. She hasn't left his side."

"That's not entirely true," I said. "She got out of the limo for a few minutes, and then when I went around and offered people coffee she came out of the dressing room and got pop."

"It's so cute that you say pop," Eldridge said.

"Stop it."

"Would that be enough time to shoot up?" Louis asked. Then he hit a button on the blender and none of us could speak for almost thirty seconds.

When the blender stopped, I said, "I don't think any of us would know how long it takes to shoot up. But I'm guessing no. I mean, from the movies I've seen, he'd have to get out his syringe, and a rubber tube for tying off his arm, and a spoon and a lighter, and then the heroin in a tiny baggie, which he'd have to heat up in the spoon... Yeah, no. I don't think his manager was out of the room long enough."

"Not to mention," Eldridge said. "After he shot up he'd have to put everything away really quick, but he'd be high, which would make it hard to do, wouldn't it?"

"Right," I said, a little bit impressed by him.

"I'm going to take this out to Keely," Louis said. "And maybe apologize. At least it looks like it will taste good – it's mostly passion fruit, banana, coconut milk and pineapple. And the secret powder, of course."

Before he could leave, I asked, "Did you notice Heston True's eyes?"

"You mean the fact that they're identical to Finn Henderson's," Louis said very casually.

"What?" Eldridge asked. "I didn't—they both have blue eyes?"

"The same, distinctive blue eyes," Marc said.

"Okay, wait a minute," Eldridge said. "Mikey said you guys like to try and figure out murders. But this is genetics. Do you know something about genetics?"

"You don't need a doctorate in biology to figure out when a teenager doesn't look like his father," Louis said. "Excuse me."

He left the room.

"Does it make any difference if the True kid is actually Finn Henderson's son?" Eldridge asked.

"Supposedly, Finn is in recovery. It might explain why he had a slip," I said. "I mean, either he knew and he's nervous about meeting his kid, or he didn't know and he just figured it out."

"Not to mention it would explain the tension between Finn and Kathleen," Marc said. "You did notice that, didn't you?"

"I think they noticed it on the moon."

I put a couple of cans of 7-Up onto the tray and two cups of ice. I decided against coffee. A cup of tea might be good, but first Finn needed to drink the soda. I was also hoping he'd stopped puking.

Eldridge said, "I should probably go check the table. See if anything needs to be refilled."

"And I need to go watch Keely pretend to be White," Marc said.

We all left the craft room and went our separate ways. I went back to the Zola Emery dressing room and tapped on the door. I didn't wait for anyone to say enter, since I was afraid Amber might not let me in. When I walked in, Finn was on the sofa. While I was gone his pants had been removed. He wore a pair of tighty-whities that didn't conceal much of anything. Amber was closing up a big leather handbag.

"What do you want?"

"I brought some 7-Up to help settle Finn's stomach."

"Mr. Henderson, please," she said.

That seemed awfully formal for someone I'd just watched throw up. Still, I said, "Okay... Mr. Henderson."

I set the tray down on the makeup table and poured out a cup of soda. "I brought one for you as well, Ms. Bright."

"No, thank you," she said. She stood there with her arms crossed seeming to assess Finn as she did.

I brought over a cup of pop and tried to hand it to him.

Instead of the cup, he grabbed my arm and said, "You have to help me. She's trying to kill me."

I looked back at Amber. She rolled her eyes and said, "It's not the first time he's said that. He doesn't mean me."

I pulled away and stood up. "Do you know who he does mean?"

"Hard to say. A mermaid, the wicked witch, a Valkyrie, his mother, one of the furies, the queen of the Martians, Joan Rivers, Zola Emery's ghost… His delusions are vivid but not especially specific."

"I heard Finn, uh… Mr. Henderson saying he wanted to fire you," I said. "What was that about?"

"Excuse me?"

"Right after we got here, through the door, I heard you say something about him firing you."

"You were listening at the door? What kind of person—"

"I was walking by. Your voice carries."

My bet was that she'd heard that before, because it was true. She took a deep, annoyed breath. "Don't pay any attention to that. He threatens to fire me all the time. He knows he can't actually do it. Not contractually. If he could, I don't think he'd threaten me like that."

"Was it something specific though? A reason he wanted to fire you tonight?"

"Excuse me, but I think you're here to get us snacks. So why don't you go take care of that."

"Um, yeah, of course…"

I was still holding the soda that Finn hadn't taken. I went to set it on the counter before leaving, but she apparently reconsidered, saying, "Look, don't say anything to the others, but he didn't want to be here. I pushed him into it. I thought it would make a good counterpoint to all the stories about what a druggie he is. And it would have… if he'd stayed sober."

"Do you know who gave him drugs?"

"I wish I did, but I can't figure it out."

"Did it happen before he got to the studio?"

"He was fine in the limo. You don't need to—"

"You left him alone with the driver. The driver could have had the drugs. Finn could have—"

"If the driver gave it to him, he didn't take it. I'd have noticed the difference in his behavior. That's enough, okay?"

"Of course. None of my business. But let's say the driver did give it to him. He was alone in here when you came out to get a Diet Coke. Could he have shot up or whatever then?"

"Not enough time," she said, confirming what we'd already decided.

"Were there any other times you left him alone?"

"I was with him the whole time."

Meanwhile, Finn had begun to babble… "Officer, officer, I had no idea there were drugs in the bag. When we got to the house my friend made me go in. I didn't want to. They gave me the bag and said I knew what to do with it. But I didn't know. I had no idea. And those guys… I don't know who they were. I barely know what they looked like. I was too afraid to look at them."

I looked at Amber who said, "Lines from one of his movies. I don't even remember which one. I don't imagine he does either."

I picked up the 7-Up and offered it to him again. "You should try to drink this."

This time he took the drink. "Is it a magic potion?"

"Sorry. It's not," I said. "We ran out of magic potions."

He nodded like that made sense and took a sip of the pop. I hoped it helped him.

I tried to get back to what he might have taken. "It couldn't have been something he just swallowed—"

"That's enough. Get out."

"Okay."

As I reached the door, she added, "And keep your mouth shut. Don't get any ideas about selling any stories to the tabloids. You try any bullshit like that and I'll make your life a living hell."

"Good to know."

I stepped out of the dressing room and closed the door behind me. Okay, that was weird. I brought a sick guy a pop to settle his stomach and ended up getting threatened with absolute destruction. I really should have asked more questions about this job.

I nearly walked away. I probably should have. But... well, I'd confronted killers in the past, not always deliberately, but I had. So what did I really have to be afraid of? Finn really should see a doctor. There was no question about that. Someone needed to make that happen, and since Amber obviously wasn't going to and I was right near the D.W. Griffith Memorial Office, which had a telephone, I thought why not me?

Just a few footsteps later, I was standing in the office behind the desk staring at an old-fashioned, black desk phone. I picked up the receiver and dialed 911. Nothing. I hadn't used a rotary phone in, like, forever. Did I not remember how to work it? I pressed down the little knobs in the cradle—they have a name, I just don't remember it. I waited for a dial tone. Nothing happened. I tried again. Nothing. I tried a few more times. Well, a lot more times.

Finally, I admitted to myself the phone was dead. I followed the cord from the back of the phone, over the edge of the desk, and down to the phone jack on the baseboard. At first it looked all right. Then I gave the cord a little tug. It came away easily. It had been cut.

ELEVEN

I walked down to the craft room to get rid of the tray I'd used to bring Finn a drink. I felt like I should do something, but I couldn't think exactly what. Running around screaming that something sinister was happening was certainly a possibility, but I wasn't exactly sure of what, why or how sinister. Still, I needed to do something.

My first thought was to tell Louis or Marc the phone line had been cut, but in all honesty, there wasn't much they could do about it. Then I remembered Kathleen had asked to be informed if I thought Finn was using. Well, not asked, commanded. I thought it wasn't nice to tattle on him—though actually, only children worried about being a tattletale, right? Grownups should be able to handle the truth. No matter who it comes from.

I tapped on the door to the Arbuckle room. Heston again opened the door but kept it nearly shut. "Go away. We don't need any more drinks."

"Can I talk to your mom?"

"No. She's busy."

"Oh, for God's sake, Heston, let the man in."

Heston stepped back and I walked into the dressing room.

Before I could say anything, Kathleen asked, "Are they ready for me? How did Finn do?"

"He didn't get through the whole thing."

"Why not?"

"It seems he got his hands on some drugs."

"Where? Who gave them to him?"

"I don't know."

"Probably that horrible manager of his."

I said, "Well, she seemed genuinely concerned. And it *is* her livelihood if he loses his career. The thing is, I tried to call an ambulance, but the phone isn't working. Someone cut—"

"Why would you call an ambulance?"

"Well... I mean, I think he's overdosed."

"Is he conscious?"

"Yes."

"Then he hasn't overdosed. He's just high. He'd be very upset if you called an ambulance when he didn't need you to."

Okay, that was a bit weird. Why did no one seem to want to help this guy?

"I still think he should see a doctor. He's delusional. He said, 'She's trying to kill me.'"

"She? He thinks his manager is trying to kill him?"

"It was a more general she."

"But you do think he meant his manager? Right?"

"I don't know what to think." And then I realized he could have meant Kathleen. Her motive was sitting on the couch. Of course, it was all ridiculous. The only person trying to kill Finn was Finn.

"You're right," she said, "We shouldn't make assumptions. We'll pray for Finn, of course." She could have sounded a little more sincere. "It *is* disappointing. I'd hoped for more."

"You shouldn't have been hoping for anything, Kathleen," her son said. "He doesn't have anything to do with us. Does he?"

"He's an old friend. Someday you'll have old friends, Heston, and you'll know what it's like when they disappoint you."

Heston just scowled at her, and said, "I'm hungry. I'm gonna get something to eat." He skulked out of the dressing room.

I stood there wondering if maybe she was right. I could be over-reacting. I seemed to be doing that a lot lately. I said, "His manager said he'll be sober in an hour or two. It's still possible he might not—disappoint you, as much—"

"I'm not the type to entertain false hopes."

I bit my tongue. I mean, that was her basic product, wasn't it? False hope? Offering people hope where there was none. And then getting them to send in money to prove their hope? Well, hating people was a big part of what she was selling. I tried to decide which was her real product: hatred or false hope. Neither was very nice.

Abruptly she asked, "Why are you still here? Go tell them I'm ready when they are."

Self-consciously, I walked out of the room. When I stepped into the hallway, I stood there for a moment gathering myself. Apparently, I didn't need to worry about Finn. He was going to be fine. It was still worrying that that the phone line had been cut, but that could have happened long before we got there. The last group to use the soundstage could have done it. Or the one before that. I decided I'd better deliver Kathleen's message and then find Louis.

"Yum, Jungle Juice," Keely was saying into the camera when I walked back onto the stage area. Then she gave the biggest, most insincere smile I'd ever seen. Well, in person. After all, I did live through the Reagan years.

After a slight pause, Donald said, "Cut! That was perfect."

"It was," Wendy added. "Good job, Keely."

I hovered just behind them, in front of the gameshow desk. They'd moved over to the yellow curtain in the center of the stage. A wise choice, as Keely looked lovely in front of it.

I wanted to give Donald Kathleen's message, but he was busy talking with Ed, who was saying, "Don't you think that guy needs to go to the emergency room?"

"No, he'll be fine. He's just high."

"People who are that high aren't fine. I think he needs a doctor."

"You're just here to carry things, Ed. Can you try to remember that?"

I began to say, "The telephone—" when Donald asked Keely, "Are you ready to continue?"

She nodded.

Stepping a foot or two back, I glanced around. I didn't see Heston. He'd said he wanted something to eat, but he wasn't at the craft table. Had he been and gone already? I checked the rest of the soundstage. Several people were slouched in the front row of the audience section. Donald, Ed and Wendy were all busy filming Keely.

Eldridge stood dutifully next to the craft table. He smiled at me, and everything seemed to stop for a moment. No, no, no—that was bad. The last thing I needed in my life was a guy who smiled, and then things around me stopped! I'd had that with Javier O'Shea, and boy did that not turn out okay. He was conflicted and a mess. And much darker than I wanted... or needed... or, whatever. Eldridge was smart and happy and normal. Stop it, I told myself, I was not making a comparison to choose between them. I'd rejected Javier and said no to going on a date with Eldridge. Everything was decided. I was happily single and planning to stay that way.

But—that smile.

It was late, almost two o'clock, maybe. I was beyond tired and a lot anxious, and shouldn't be thinking about anyone's smile. Louis was moving things around on the table, but really everything was full and, for the moment at least, people didn't seem very interested in eating. They were all watching Keely.

"Tell us about yourself, Keely," Donald said. "Who are you today?"

"Well, I have my own florist shop in Leimert Park. I'm up at six in the morning so I can be at the flower market in downtown

LA by eight. I'm back in time to open my store, where I work until eight or nine at night. Six days a week. I do get a little help from a couple of at-risk teenagers who work at the shop part-time. I love it though; flowers offer such an opportunity for creativity..."

"And your love life?" Donald asked. "Still carrying a flame for anyone we know?"

"You're not putting that in, Donald."

"Cut," he said, and clicked the button off. Though why he felt like he had to say 'cut' when he was running the camera was questionable. "Keely, what's the problem?"

"You're not reviving that storyline. It wasn't true then and it's not true now."

"Me thinks the lady doth protest too much."

"Donald. I was a teenage Black girl and you made up a story about my having a crush on a pretty White boy. Do you have any idea how much hate mail I got? From White people *and* Black people. You want to talk about that on camera? You want to talk about how you made up a story and people hated me for it? I'll gladly talk about that—"

"I don't think that's what OTN wants."

"Then leave it alone."

"All right, fine. But you did have a crush on Finn."

"And if I did... you thought it was okay to exploit a young girl's feelings?"

"Do you need a break, Keely?" Wendy asked.

"Let's just go on."

Wendy gave her a husband a look that clearly meant 'get on with it.'

Louis stepped over to me and whispered, "If I'd known this was going to be so dramatic, I would have made popcorn and left it at that." Then he asked, "How is Finn Henderson?"

"High. Very high. Delusional even. And the telephone's dead."

"What?"

"All right. Quiet everyone. Action!" Donald called out before pressing the button on the camera. He waited three beats, then, "So... Keely can you tell us some of your favorite memories of the show?"

"I remember this one time, Kathleen got invited to a Halloween party at a USC frat house. She and Finn stole some costumes and makeup from this high school pilot that was shooting on the stage next to us, and went as the king and queen of the prom who got killed in a car crash on the way. It was funny."

"What did you go as?"

"Oh, I didn't go. It was the late seventies. Black girls didn't go to frat parties held by rich White boys. I wasn't exactly safe."

"Could we try that again," Donald said. "Just say you didn't feel well." A moment later, he asked, "What did you go as?"

"Oh, I didn't go. I wasn't feeling well. I was coming down with syphilis."

Donald left a beat. I was pretty sure none of that would get in. After the beat, he asked, "Do you have a story that's... more about you?"

Keely looked like she might snap at him for a moment, then said, "Why don't I take a break and I'll think of one. Does that work for you, Donald?"

"We only have so much time, you realize. And we're not getting as much as I hoped we would..."

Louis pulled me back toward the table, and asked, "What do you mean the phone is dead?"

"I mean the phone is dead." He gave me a frustrated look, so I added. "I thought someone should call an ambulance for Finn. I mean, no one else seems to think so, but—"

"It doesn't matter if you couldn't get through."

"Someone cut the cord."

Louis had a very concerned look on his face.

"I'll go while Keely takes a break," Grace said to Donald.

I looked over and she was already smoothing her outfit,

which was a very expensive, overly tailored suit with a gray, knee length skirt, a matching blazer with subtle shoulder pads, and beneath that she wore a collarless black silk blouse. Over it all lay a double strand of pearls. She looked a lot like she did on the back of a bus bench.

"Louis! We need Grace's drink."

"On it," he said, walking away.

Grace climbed onto the stool. Donald and Ed spent a couple of minutes moving the camera so that the angle would be different than the one they'd used for Keely.

I looked for another window to tell Donald that Kathleen was ready. I edged closer and tried to get his attention, but he was too involved with the camera to notice me.

"Um, Donald—"

He turned and snapped at me, "Don't you have something you can be doing?"

"Actually, I'm trying—"

"Do I look fat?" Grace asked. "No one wants a fat real estate agent. At least not a woman."

"You look lovely, Grace," Wendy said.

"Thank you."

"Donald—"

He turned and snapped at me. "No one wants a soda. All right?"

"Um, that's not—"

"And where is Grace's Juicy Juice? Can you find out?"

"Louis went to make it two seconds ago," I said. I took a deep breath, about to try again to tell Donald—

"Quiet! Everyone quiet. We're going to start."

"Donald, we don't have the Juicy Juice."

"It's okay, we'll circle back. Grace. When you're ready."

Donald said, "Action." Pause. "Tell us about your life, Grace."

"Well, I'm a top real estate agent catering to Hollywood's elite. I focus on Brentwood, Beverly Hills, Bel-Air and the

Pacific Palisades. My sales last year topped twenty million dollars."

"So, I guess you don't miss being an actress?"

"Well, the thing is… The lessons I learned as an actress I put to use every day. The purchase or sale of a million-dollar home can require me to take on many roles: best friend, financial advisor, parent, therapist, teacher, confidant… The last thing anyone wants is for me to be myself."

She smiled at the camera. A smile that seemed very much like the fake smile she probably showed to her clients.

"So, right after the show you became a real estate agent?"

She hesitated, and then said, "Yes, that's exactly right. The moment the show ended I became a real estate agent."

"You must have been a very young real estate agent."

"Well, all right… It took me a few years to get my footing after the show. But all young people go through trying periods."

And then Louis was there, handing Grace her drink.

"Cut!" Donald called out.

"Oh, sorry," Louis said. Then to Grace he said, "Summer Passion."

"What?" Grace said, seeming almost offended.

"That's what the drink is called," Louis said. "It's a lot of passion fruit."

Grace carefully positioned the logo so it could be seen on camera and refrained from taking a sip. She waited patiently while Donald gathered himself. "Ready?"

"Yes."

"All right, then. Action." He pressed the button on the camera. "Grace, you were telling us about your life."

"Let me take a sip of the juice," Grace corrected him.

"Oh, yeah, that."

"There's no dairy in this is there? Or any kind of fat?"

"Absolutely not," Wendy said from the sidelines. I wondered how true that was. I was pretty sure whey was a kind of milk product. I remembered a nursery rhyme about curds and whey, so there was—

Grace took a sip of the drink, and said, "Oh, it's so good!" She smiled, held the smile for several beats, then said, "I'm not going to be able to drink that. I'm sorry… It's just—no."

"Just hold the cup, dear," Wendy said.

"Let's try that again," Donald said. "And leave a pause before you comment. I have to edit this."

Suddenly, Wendy crumpled to the floor. I was closest to her, so I got there first. I was getting down onto the floor with her, but she was already recovering.

"I'm fine! I'm fine! There's nothing to worry about." She sat up. "I couldn't find my medication. I'm sure I put the bottle in my purse, but when I went to find it, it wasn't there."

"Wendy, is this your purse over here?" Meg asked. "Would you like me to take another look for your pills?"

"Oh, would—"

"No," Donald said. To his wife, he said, "You don't want random people pawing through your things."

"It's not like I have secrets, Donald." Looking back to Meg, she said, "If you don't mind, dear. Lately I can't see things right in front of me."

"Is there anything that would help while we're looking for your pills?" I asked. "Water?"

"Oh, water would be wonderful. Thank you."

I walked over to the table. "Is there any evian out here?" I asked Eldridge.

He shook his head and asked if I wanted him to go get some.

"No, that's okay. I'll do it."

I walked to the far end of the stage, passing Keely and Meg—who were deep in Wendy's purse. Getting to the back hallway, I walked by the empty office, the Emery room. I thought I heard the sound of Amber crying, which made me wonder if Finn actually had fired her. Passing the Durante room, I saw Ricky had taken off his shirt and was flexing for himself in the still smudgy mirror. Then I reached the craft room. Once inside I grabbed an armful of evians, and started back the way I'd come.

This time Ricky saw me glance into his dress room.

"Like what you see?" he called out.

"Um... sorry."

I had no idea how he expected me to answer that question. As I walked by the Emery room, I listened hard to see if I could hear Amber still crying, when I smelled cigarette smoke. It seemed to be coming from the men's room. I opened the door to find Marc in there.

"What are you doing in here?"

"Smoking. What does it look like I'm doing?"

"Wendy passed out because she can't find her meds."

"This is a nightmare."

"Have you heard Amber crying in Finn's dressing room?"

"No, but it wouldn't surprise me. Women tend to cry around Finn. A lot."

"Oh." He was suggesting something I hadn't thought of. "You really think so? She seemed all business to me."

"That's probably why she's taking it hard. She thought she had a deal." The word deal got air quotes.

"The telephone's dead," I said.

"Of course it is. I just want to go home. I'm sorry we involved you in this mess."

"It's okay. We're getting paid."

"Don't hold your breath."

"Oh."

With that, I left to bring Wendy a bottle of water. When I got back to the stage, she'd been helped over to one of the audience seats next to Meg and Keely. Donald and Ed were all set to start filming again. I went over to Wendy and gave her the bottle of evian. She actually did look better. I wondered what was wrong with her.

Looking around for Louis, I couldn't find him. I wondered where he went to. I was just in the backstage area so—

"Quiet everyone. And... action." Donald said, as he pushed the button on the camera.

After a beat, he asked, "Grace, did you have a crush on Finn like the other girls?"

She sidestepped that question by saying, "We all knew Finn was going places. Being with Finn was as much about being seen with him as it was about actually spending time with him."

"So, you did hope to continue your acting career after *Kapowie!*"

"Not for long. Things... Well, things were difficult. And then..."

Suddenly, the air on the soundstage seemed to change. Things became stoney silent. I looked over to see Kathleen and Heston suddenly standing there. He must have found his way back to the dressing room at some point. That's when I noticed a look passing between Kathleen and Grace. A look that was every bit as passionate as angry, and as hate-filled as the look that had recently passed between Kathleen and Finn.

Not for the first time, I thought, *Weird stuff is happening. Really weird stuff.*

TWELVE

Kathleen looked around, taking it all in. Then, seeing me, she said, "Didn't you tell them I was ready?"

"Well, I tried... but, they were shooting—"

"Always interrupt for Kathleen," Donald said with a snarl.

"Well, I did actually, but you wouldn't let me—"

Ignoring me, he said to Grace. "You've done wonderfully, Grace. Thank you so much."

"I'm not sure I was finished," she said stiffly.

"I'm hoping there will be some time for pickups before we all go home." Angrily, Grace got off the stool. As she did, Kathleen said, "You're not shooting me against yellow. I'll look like a harpy. Set me up in front of the red curtain."

Wendy got up from her seat and came over, saying, "Kathleen, you look so lovely."

Heston came over to the craft table and started asking, "What is this?" about everything except the M&Ms. Eldridge patiently explained. Then the kid asked, "Is there gonna be, like, actual breakfast?"

Louis appeared behind me, answering, "We're going to make omelets in about an hour." And by that he meant *he* was going to make them. I mean, I could make an omelet. It just wouldn't be pretty.

"Where did you go?" I asked.

Lowering his voice, he said, "I wanted to take a look at the doors. I got one of them to budge about an eighth of an inch. But it seemed like I was just making it worse."

"They're really jammed shut."

"Do you buy Donald's explanation?" he asked me.

"You mean that he's not paying to use the soundstage? I guess. I don't know. How much do places like this cost?"

He shrugged. "Five or ten thousand a day, I'd guess."

"Oh yeah, he's not paying for this."

"Do you think they're paying Finn for drinking their drink?"

"Definitely. That would be where the money went."

Louis pondered a moment, and said, "You know this might be a good time for more coffee. Can you fill a pot and bring it out here?"

Before I could answer, Wendy called out, "Louis! Make Kathleen a Blue Moon."

"Oh please, no," Kathleen said. "Could you make me a Green Goddess?"

Wendy flushed, excited. "Oh my, you've been to one of our stores? So, you're a fan?"

"I sent an assistant for a menu."

"Oh—that works too. Louis!"

"Yes, I heard."

"Um, I'll have the Blue Moon," Heston said through a mouth full of shortbread.

"Got it," Louis said, then he and I walked over to the craft room. As we went, I asked, "Isn't Green Goddess a kind of dressing?"

"It is. I'd have picked a different name."

"And how is it different from a Giant Green Monster?"

"Different fruits and veggies. Apples and carrots, but the rest is the same."

As we reached the craft services room, Marc and Grace came out holding cups of coffee. That was two I didn't have to refill.

"What's going on out there?" Marc asked.

"Kathleen is going to give it a try," I said.

"I think she'll do just fine," Louis said. "I suspect that the network will be happy with whatever she says."

"Oh yeah, she'll give them what they want," Grace said bitterly. "I don't think she believes a word of what she says on TV. It's all showbiz to her."

Somehow that made it all worse. She said really hateful things just to be popular. I asked Grace, "Have you been down to see Finn?"

"God, no. We're hardly friends."

"Oh. I thought you said you sold him a house?"

"Two actually. But that's not friendship, that's business. Come on Marc, let's go have a quick cigarette."

As they walked away, Louis said pointedly, "Someone's smoking a lot."

With a raised eyebrow, Marc said, "Someone knew what he was getting into, so he brought two packs."

"Oh dear," Louis said before we stepped into the craft room. He started making the Green Goddess, while I filled a coffee pot from the urn.

"I found sugar packets and little creamers in that drawer, there," he said. "I prefer actual cream, but it's too hard to serve."

"It's your first time," I said.

"And last. I could not do this for a living. It's one thing to have people tell you what to do. It's another to have idiots tell you what to do."

As far as I knew, he just described most work situations. And I'd have to include my store, in which case I was the idiot telling people what to do. Much more pleasant for me but probably not anyone else. I filled my pockets with sugar and creamers, and said, "Well, see you out there."

In the hallway, I walked down and tapped on the door for the

Emery dressing room. Before I could say anything, Amber screamed, "Go away!"

So, I did. Then I looked into the Durante room. Ricky was still in there, still shirtless. But now he was holding a mobile phone with its antenna fully extended. He was waving it around toward the ceiling. He noticed me standing there, and said, "I'm not getting any bars."

I had no idea what that meant. Cellular phones were far too expensive for me to even think about. I asked, "Can I get you anything?"

"Is there a telephone around here?"

"There's one in the office, but it doesn't work."

"It doesn't work? What do you mean it doesn't work?"

"I mean, it doesn't work."

Why do people ask questions that have obvious answers?

He brushed by me on his way to see for himself. I was tempted to ask who he wanted to call at nearly three in the morning, when he looked over his shoulder and answered the unasked question, "I promised my girlfriend I'd call her."

Somehow, I doubted that. Given Ricky's history with tabloids, it seemed likely the phone call would be to report Finn Henderson's most recent overdose. Having a photographer outside the studio to get a shot of him leaving in the morning would be very valuable. No doubt, Ricky wanted to sell the information. Of course, that made me wonder if Donald had cut the phone line for this very reason? To protect Finn.

Glancing down the hall, I saw that Louis had finished the Green Goddess and the Blue Moon, and was hurrying back out to the stage with them. I walked down and checked the other dressing rooms. They were empty.

When I got out to the stage, Louis was giving Kathleen her drink, while Donald and Wendy fussed over her. Ed was standing around again, though he must have helped move and set up the camera while I was in the back. Heston was sipping his drink and nibbling off the craft table as Eldridge looked on, clearly bored. He brightened when he saw me, though. That was a little scary. I immediately turned toward Keely and Meg, who were still sitting in the front row of the risers.

"Oh no, they're not really at-risk kids. They're actually honor students," Keely was saying. "I just said at-risk because I knew it would fit what Donald thinks of Black folk."

I asked if they'd like more coffee.

"I'd kill for a cup of coffee," Keely said.

"Oh yes, more," Meg said, holding out her cup. "I hope it's okay. I helped myself earlier."

"It's fine. The coffee's there to be drunk."

"It's really good coffee," Meg said.

And that's when I realized I didn't have any cups and needed one for Keely. I refilled Meg's cup, then said to Keely, "It'll just be a minute and I'll have a cup for you."

I went over to the table and asked Eldridge to run back to the craft room and get coffee cups. I mean, I'd just come from there —God, I was terrible at this.

Donald yelled out, "Quiet please, we're going to give this a try." Things went quiet. Then Donald politely asked Kathleen, "Are you ready, Kathleen?"

She nodded. I had to admit she looked amazing in front of the red curtain. The lights made a halo around her giant wig, making her look like a saintly hooker.

"Well, Kathleen, tell the fans at home about your life today."

Her smile registered at about 200 watts. "Shortly after *Kapowie!* ended, I was in a terrible place. Drinking, taking drugs, going with men. If there was sin around, I was in. And then, one Sunday morning, I was drinking wine at eleven in the morning, watching television. Nothing was on, so I was going from one channel to the next, and that was when I saw him: Reverend Winthrop True. The way he spoke... it was like he was speaking only to me. The next Sunday I went to his church in Orange

County, Victory Covenant. I met the reverend during fellowship and, as they say, 'the rest is history.'"

"When did you first feel a calling to the Lord?"

"Oh, always. I didn't know what it was at first, and like other teenage girls I wanted to be cool. Unfortunately, Jesus wasn't cool. At least not to the people I knew. But then I found out that Jesus *is* cool. That Jesus is the *coolest*. Once I learned that, I could let my true self out."

Donald waited a moment, and then said, "Cut" as he turned off the camera. "That was just terrific, Kathleen."

She took a sip of her drink, carefully through a straw so as not to mess up her lipstick.

I noticed Marc and Grace coming out and joining Keely and Meg in the audience. Then Eldridge was back, handing me a short stack of Styrofoam coffee cups. I took a couple, then said, "You can put the rest on the table." I poured a cup for Keely and brought it over.

Very quietly, Marc said, "At least she's not talking about the evil gays."

"Not yet, anyway," Keely said.

Behind me, I heard Kathleen saying, "Wendy, this drink is delicious. Thank you."

"Kathleen," Wendy said, in what I'd call her reasonable voice. "As you're speaking, if you could pause and take sip, making sure that the store's logo faces the camera."

Kathleen glared at her harshly for just a moment, then she turned on that smile. "Of course I can." She took another sip of the drink, obviously enjoying it. "And as soon as I'm done, we'll talk about a donation to Victory Covenant."

Even without seeing her face, I knew Wendy blanched. Or at least her shoulders froze and her whole body stiffened. She'd made a tactical mistake. Kathleen was going to endorse Juicy Juice, but Donald and Wendy had no idea how much that was going to cost them. I had the feeling it would cost them quite a lot.

"Well, then, perhaps we should continue," Donald said. "Quiet everyone." We'd been quiet. It was too interesting to watch Kathleen and Wendy. "Action!"

"Kathleen, can you tell us a favorite memory of your time on *Kapowie!*"

She left a long pause; I assumed for editing purposes. Then Kathleen said, "At Victory Covenant we have a program for troubled teens. It's deeply influenced by my time on *Kapowie!* I come in and teach the kids some of the songs we used to sing. I especially like the song 'You Are the Light'. Do you remember that one? I know it sounds like it's about finding yourself, so typical of the Me Generation. But I think it's about finding God inside you. Because he's there. He's inside all of us. All you have to do is look."

She stopped talking and waited. Finally, Donald said, "Cut!" as he turned off the camera.

"Donald, I'm just thinking... When Finn feels better, can we get the entire cast together and sing 'You Are the Light'? I think it would be lovely to include that."

"We'd probably have to cancel the dance number — are you saying we *should* cancel the dance number?" Wendy asked.

"Well, it has been an awfully long time since we danced together. Singing as a group might be a bit easier and help us get through this long, long night."

"Sure, we can give that a try," Donald says. "It would have to be a cappella, of course."

"Well, yes, that's true. It could be a good segue into a clip from the original show where we sang it with instruments. Actually, I think we sang that song five times, didn't we? Different costumes. Different singers highlighted."

"You're right, Kathleen," Wendy said. "We did rely on that song a lot."

"Because it's just so wonderful!"

She took a sip of her drink and made gurgling noises. "Oh, look at that. I drank the whole thing."

"Can I have another one made for you?" Wendy asked.

"I really shouldn't."

Kathleen was biting her lip, deciding about a second drink, when the television popped on and a video began to play. Obviously someone had a remote, but looking around the room I couldn't see exactly who.

Turning back to the screen it looked very dark. I could barely make out what I was looking at. It appeared to have been shot through a window. There was a couple in a room making out. Other people seemed to be picking this up before I did, because they began saying things like "Oh my God," and "What the—"

And then the couple's faces caught the light. It was Finn; the man was Finn. And the woman was Kathleen. Even though the video quality was terrible, it was still easy to see they weren't teenagers. This had been shot recently. Very recently. As soon as that thought formed, Kathleen was screaming, "No! Who took that? Who's behind this? Donald, make it stop!"

"Okay, where's the remote? Who's got it?"

Everyone was looking around, while Kathleen screamed, "Stop! It has to stop!"

Then, suddenly, the TV went off. Ed had disconnected the power. Kathleen stood there with her hands on her face. After a moment, she dropped them and smiled at us all.

"Okay, okay, easy to explain. Two old friends, greeting each other..."

"Seriously?" Keely said. "I wouldn't mind an old friend like that."

"Fine. It *is* what it looks like. But we're all sinners, aren't we?"

"And some sinners are hypocrites," Marc said.

"Judge not, lest ye be judged."

"Gimme a break. All you do is judge people."

"Well, maybe I need to think about that. Does anyone know if this is an original tape or if it's a copy? And if it's a copy, who has the original?"

Just then, Amber walked onto the stage. She was saying

something nearly inaudible. Two syllables. That was all I picked up.

"What did you say?" Wendy asked.

Then Amber took a deep, ragged breath, and screamed, "He's dead!"

THIRTEEN

Oh God, oh God, oh God. Another dead person! I couldn't believe I was there again... My heart was racing, I'd broken out in a sweat, and I wasn't entirely sure I was breathing. Around me was chaos. Everyone was talking at once. No one was making sense. Kathleen was wailing.

"This is a disaster," Donald gasped. "An absolute disaster... I'll lose everything!"

"Does anyone know first aid?" Louis wanted to know.

"I know some," Ed said. "Do you think he's *not* dead? Could that be possible?"

"Let's make sure she hasn't made a mistake," Louis said.

"Can someone call an ambulance?" Ed called out.

"The phone isn't working," I said. "Oh my God, the phone isn't working!"

Ed gave me a worried look as he and Louis hurried off the stage.

"The phone isn't working?" Grace said, coming over to me. "You mean the desk phone in the office?"

"Yeah, uh-huh, the line was cut."

"No one panic," Donald said. "Everything's under control."

"What do you mean everything's under control?! Nothing's

under control!" Keely screeched. Donald's attempt at avoiding panic was causing panic. "Oh my God. Oh my God…"

"We have to get help," Meg said, putting her arm around Keely.

At that point, I noticed Eldridge standing next to me. He whispered, "You're going to be fine."

Everything seemed to stop for a moment. He was right. I was going to be fine. I didn't know Finn. He wasn't a friend of mine. He was just the dead person in the next room. Things like this happen to everyone. Okay, they happen to me more often, but still—

"STOP! For God's sake. Everyone, STOP," Amber was yelling. She wiped the tears from her face, and with determination said, "It doesn't matter if the phone works or not. We're *not* calling an ambulance. We're *not* calling the police."

"I have to say I agree with Ms. Bright," Donald said, his voice shaky but basically calm.

"What? Are you both crazy?" I said. "This is *exactly* the time you call the police. I mean… if we could."

"It's not what Finn would have wanted," Amber said.

"No, it's definitely not what he'd have wanted," Donald parroted.

"He's dead. I don't think he gets a vote," Marc said.

"Really Marc?" Meg said. "Now is not the time to be funny."

"I wasn't trying to be funny. That was a fact, not a joke."

"I… I have a plan," Amber said. "All we have to do is get his body back to his house. There's a call girl he's fond of, Arabella. I know she'll go there, and *she* can call the police. She can say she woke up next to him after a night of sex and drugs, and discovered him dead."

"What are you talking about?" I asked. "Why would you do that?"

"Finn has an image to maintain. There's no way I'm letting him die of an overdose on a broken-down soundstage recording a show about a bunch of has-beens and never-weres."

"Now, wait just a minute," Donald said. "That's a bit harsh, to say the least."

Ignoring him, I said, "Dead people don't have images to maintain. What you're saying is crazy."

"Elvis. Marilyn Monroe. James Dean. Their estates make millions. Just because Finn is gone doesn't mean his career dies with him. It's important to make the right choice about what happens next."

Okay, I was wrong. Dead people did have images to maintain.

"If you want our help, you maybe shouldn't refer to us as has-beens and never-weres," Keely pointed out.

Ignoring her, Amber turned to Marc and said, "Explain to me why we can't leave now? What's wrong with the doors?"

"They're locked," Marc said. "Well, jammed. Deliberately."

"Deliberately? Donald, what's going on?"

While he hemmed and hawed, I heard Keely saying, "I can't believe it."

"I know... He's dead," Meg said, threatening another crying jag.

"Actually, I meant I can't believe that Finn and Kathleen were still seeing each other. Who would have thought?"

Then Donald began answering Amber's question. "I didn't want everyone to know this, but we're not paying for the space. We know the guard, Alan, and he let us in. Then he put doorstops into the door jambs so we couldn't get out. If the guard at the north gate knew we were here..."

And then, Louis and Ed were back looking very somber. Louis said, "Yeah, he's definitely dead."

"Thank you for confirming that," Donald said. "I think we should all—"

"I *told* you he was dead," Amber said, crossly. "Look, Donald, isn't there a way to contact the guard?"

"He's coming to let us out at seven."

"What about the giant door? The one they use to load things in?" I asked.

"It needs a key," Ed said. "The guard has it."

"We just need to remain calm," Donald said. "I think we should all take a break. It might be a good idea to move breakfast up. In about an hour we should move forward with the shoot."

"What?" Keely said. "Is that a joke? We're just going to finish filming?"

"For Finn. We'll do it as a memorial."

"I think that's disgusting," Meg said.

Donald ignored her. "We don't have enough footage yet. We should try again with Marc. Given the circumstances, I've decided to allow you greater latitude. What do you say, Marc?"

"Uh... gee thanks," Marc said, sarcastically.

"We're talking about recording a song rather than the dance number... And then Wendy and I need to tape our remembrances. So, yes, there's quite a lot to do still. But I think a break is called for."

"Finn died," Grace said. "I don't think we should continue. And we're certainly not going to *sing*."

"I'm sure he'd want the show to go on."

"I wouldn't," Keely said. "I'd want you all to be emotionally destroyed. Not that you would be..."

"I would be upset if you died," Meg said.

"Me too," Grace said.

"Okay, you don't have to..." Keely said. "My point was maybe the show *shouldn't* go on."

"Look, we can't go anywhere until seven o'clock. That's nearly four hours. You might as well finish the shoot," Amber said.

"And then what?" Grace asked. "We help you to the car with Finn's body?"

"No, no, no. As soon as I can get outside, I'll call Finn's driver. *He'll* help me with Finn's body. None of you have to do anything."

"Except keep our mouths shut," Ricky said.

"Speaking of which… I have NDAs with me that I'll be asking you each to sign."

"What's an NDA?" Meg asked.

"It's a nondisclosure agreement," I explained. I had to sign one to get the software Pinx Video runs on. Not that I actually understood the software well enough to give away any secrets. "An NDA means you won't say anything about the things that happened here tonight."

"But what if the police ask us questions?" Keely wanted to know.

"You can't say anything. *Even* if the police ask questions," Amber said. "Which they won't. So there's nothing to worry about."

"This might be a good time to mention that Amber has agreed to forgo Finn's salary if it's distributed among the rest of the cast members," Donald said. "You'll all be getting *triple* what you were promised. And… you'll be getting it before you leave, as soon as you sign the release form."

"And the NDA," Amber said. "You get the check after you sign *both* documents."

Louis came over and said to me, "Let's get breakfast going. These people need a distraction." He headed back to the craft room, while I lingered for a moment as Eldridge began removing the candy and some of the sweeter items.

"I should have asked before… You're okay, aren't you?"

"Me? Yeah, I'm fine. I mean, we're trapped in here with a dead guy. That's a new experience."

"Great," I said before I walked away. I guess that was the way to look at all of this. It was a new experience. That's all. I could deal with that. This was new; I'd never dealt with it before. It didn't even remind me—okay, it did remind me of lots of other times I was in close proximity to a corpse. I tried not to think of it that way.

In the craft room, I asked Louis, "How exactly are you going to make omelets?"

"I have a propane burner." Then he added, "Everything's all bagged up and ready to go out. I really just wanted to talk to you. What do you think is going on?"

"I don't know. I don't have a lot of experience with hard drugs or, well, any drugs really."

"It's too bad Leon's not here."

"What is there to know, though?" I asked. "He was high. Or at least, he *looked* high."

"But how fast would an overdose cause death? Does it happen right away, or does it take a while? And are there things that would look like an overdose but weren't?"

I shrugged, clueless. "We don't know when he shot up. Or even *if* he shot up. I think there are other ways to take heroin."

"Did he seem high when he got here?"

"No one really interacted with him until he was in front of the camera. That's when his manager discovered he was high. Maybe she was faking that? Maybe she... Wait, do you think Finn *didn't* overdose? We were talking before about how hard it would have been for him to shoot up without his manager knowing about it."

"She could be lying," Louis said. "She has a lot to gain by lying. Do you think she gave him drugs?"

"I brought them some pop. After he puked. When I walked into the room, she was putting something into her purse."

"I noticed that purse when we checked on him. Big, big purse. It could carry almost anything."

The way he was looking at me made me say, "Oh no. No. I'm not doing that."

"Doing what?"

"I'm not going down to Finn's dressing room to look into Amber's purse."

"Well, that's *your* idea, not mine. I have to say it's not a bad one though."

"No."

"If she did give him drugs... Well, that would be a crime—wouldn't it?"

"Which I would want nothing to do with."

"Okay, not a problem."

He picked up a TJ's bag with the burner in a box, a small frying pan, a metal bowl and four dozen eggs. In his other hand, he grabbed a second bag with omelet fillings: sliced ham, crumbled bacon, onions, spinach, tomatoes, avocado, mushrooms, salsa ... and who knows what else.

As he left the room, I said, "No," to his back. "Not gonna do it."

"Don't take too long doing what you're not going to do. I could use a hand."

For a moment I was angry. Louis assumed I was going to go down to the Zola Emery dressing room and look into Amber's bag. Actually, he knew I would. And I wouldn't be angry, except that I knew I would too. I wanted to talk myself out of it, but that wasn't going to work. I was going to do it. Finally, I told myself I should just do it and get it over with.

I hurried down the hallway to the last dressing room. After a quick tap, I opened the door and walked in. The room was empty. Well, not exactly *empty*. Finn's body was still laid out on the couch. He hadn't even been covered up. Not that I saw a blanket anywhere, but someone could have laid his pants over him.

Why wasn't he wearing pants? Had he puked on them? They were hanging on the back of a chair in front of the makeup table. I stepped over and very carefully inspected them. Fearing the worst, I held my breath. But... they looked clean. He hadn't puked on them. So why did he take them off?

The leather bag sat on the makeup table. I went over and opened it up. Right on top was a syringe. The hair on the back of my neck stood up. She *had* given him drugs. I picked up the syringe, it was plastic with black lines marking the dosage. The needle was still in it. I leaned over to look for the rest of the things you'd need to give someone heroin—the spoon, the baggie, the lighter... But there wasn't enough time.

Behind me, I heard footsteps outside the door. I jumped away from the bag and, as quietly as possible, stepped into the bathroom. I heard the door open and someone come into the dressing room.

I was trapped. I couldn't believe I'd let this happen. What if whoever this was decided they needed to pee? There was definitely no place for me to hide in the tiny bathroom.

"You son of a bitch," Amber said on the other side of the door. "How could you do this to me?"

Her? She gave him drugs? How could *she* do it to *him*? I mean, she probably thought it was part of her job, but still—she'd given him a fatal dose of drugs! That had to be a least a little bit illegal.

"Just when we were getting you back on track. The buzz on *Running Toward Justice* is amazing. There's talk of awards, Golden Globes, Oscars. And now you're... oh, oh my God..." She actually giggled. "Now you'll definitely win. You won't be here to enjoy it... but I will. I'll enjoy it. I'll be overseeing your estate. And funeral. It has to be amazing. Huge. An event. Everyone needs to be there. Everyone. I need to get started. Oh my God there's so much to do."

There was a short pause before she said, "God damn it, no bars. Isn't there... I wonder..."

And then the door to the dressing room opened and closed. She was gone. I started breathing again, not realizing I'd stopped. After a long, fretful minute, I stepped out of the bathroom and into the dressing room. Trying not to look at Finn, I noticed that the bag was no longer on the dressing table. Obviously, I wouldn't be able to finish searching it. I peeked out into the hallway. When I saw the coast was clear, I left. Just seconds later I was back in the craft room. Alone.

That's when I looked down and realized I was still holding the syringe in my hand.

FOURTEEN

The thing about death is that it's an everyday occurrence. Somewhere, generally somewhere far away, it's happening. It's normal. Except, of course, when it's you or someone you care about, then it's *not* normal. After Finn died, after I calmed down, things felt kind of normal. He was a stranger, after all. But then, he was also in a room nearby. Less than a fifty feet away. *That* definitely was not normal.

I put the syringe into one of the Trader Joe bags we'd brought with us and went out to the stage area. Louis and Eldridge had already set everything up for the omelets, and he was ready to start cooking. Which was very Louis — and so, very normal.

Donald, Ed and Ricky stood near the camera equipment. Marc and the girls hovered near the risers. Louis said loudly, "If anyone wants an omelet, come and get it." The suggestion was so normal it seemed abnormal. No one moved.

"What did you find out?" Louis asked, under his breath.

"Amber gave him the drugs."

"Oh my God," Eldridge said. "That's just like Cathy Smith."

"Who's Cathy Smith?" Louis asked.

"The woman who killed John Belushi."

"Aren't you a little young..."

"He was a very precocious eight-year-old," I explained.

"So you found drugs in her bag?"

"Just a syringe," I explained. "She came back, and I had to hide in the bathroom."

"She didn't find you?"

"No. She was too busy talking to Finn's corpse."

"Okay, that's creepy," Louis said. "Did she admit what she did?"

"Not exactly. Mostly she was just excited about how great dying is going to be for Finn's career."

"She already made that clear."

"To us," I pointed out. "Then she made it clear to Finn's corpse."

Louis shivered, then said to Eldridge. "I'm a little thirsty. Would you grab me a 7-Up from the back? And maybe bring out a selection of sodas in case anyone else wants one. And evian."

Eldridge nodded, then winked at me as he walked away. As soon as he was out of earshot, Louis said, "Thank you."

"What for?"

"Eldridge is amazing. He does everything I ask him to. So much better than Leon would have been. That was a misguided idea."

"He asked me out."

"Leon?" Louis couldn't help smirking even as he said it.

"Shut up."

"So... tell me your plans. First dates are very important. Make it memorable. My first date with Marc... Well, after we met at The Gauntlet and tricked... Our first *real* date was an afternoon at LACMA staring at beautiful paintings and then dinner at El Coyote. Followed by two blissful days of fucking."

I really wished Marc was nearer to us so he could say, "Louis!" But he wasn't so I went with, "Okay—TMI!"

He stared at me a moment, and then said, "Oh God, you told him no."

"There are so many reasons not to go out with him."

"There are always reasons *not* to do things. That doesn't mean you shouldn't do them."

"Things don't go well for me."

"Things don't go well for anyone... until they do."

"You know what I'm talking about."

"Noah, bad luck is not a personality trait. It's entirely possible—in fact, I would say likely—that nothing bad will ever happen to you again."

"Really?"

"Okay, you're right. Something bad will happen to you and me and Marc and everyone, but that doesn't mean you won't also have good things happen to you. Eldridge is a *good* thing."

I couldn't agree with that or disagree, so I kept quiet for a moment before I said, "No one's eating. How long do we have to stand here?"

"Relax. If I cook it they will come," he said.

Out of the corner of my eye, I'd been watching Donald encouraging Ed to come over and get an omelet. He walked over.

"I'm supposed to ask for an omelet, but it feels weird," Ed said. "I mean, someone died."

"Yeah, and when someone dies people eat," Louis said. "A lot. Wakes. Shivas. Casseroles. Hell, people used to eat each other's sins."

"I guess you're right. I hadn't thought about it like that."

"What would you like in your omelet?"

Ed looked back at Donald. He really had to order it whether he was going to eat it or not. "Um, I guess some cheese and maybe bacon."

"Feta or cheddar?"

"Cheddar."

Louis got to work putting butter in the pan, cracking the eggs, beating them in a metal bowl. Eldridge came back with sodas and water in a tub of ice. I wondered if I should be serving more coffee. But then Eldridge smiled at me, and I forgot what I was thinking about. Behind me, Louis flirted with Ed.

"So, how did you end up here?" Louis asked. I swear he was about to bat his eyes.

"I started working at the Juicy Juice in North Hollywood."

"Recently? So, you don't know the Barclays well?"

"No, I don't. I mean, they seem nice."

That wasn't exactly the word I'd use. But then Donald was only thirty feet away, so it wouldn't be wise to use the word I *would* use.

"I'm surprised they don't have you making the juice drinks," Louis said.

"Somebody's gotta carry stuff."

"Ah... One of life's basic rules: Somebody's gotta carry stuff. What did you do before Juicy Juice?"

He shrugged. "I was learning to be a carpenter, but I haven't been able to get on anywhere since the quake. Foundations are where it's at. But I don't know anything about concrete."

I'd never thought of concrete as a difficult subject.

In a very showy move, Louis flipped the omelet. Eldridge handed him a paper plate and he slid the omelet onto it. I picked up some plastic cutlery wrapped in a paper napkin with a blue ribbon on it and handed it to Ed.

When he took it, I noticed that there was a blurry tattoo at the base of his thumb: five dots, like the number five from a pair of dice. I wondered what that meant.

"Take a soda if you'd like," Louis said. "Or I can make you a Juicy Juice?"

"A Juicy Juice isn't really a treat for me. I'll just grab a soda."

After picking out a soda, Ed walked back over to the camera and sat down on the case it came in. He seemed to deflate the minute he sat.

I said to Louis, "You're a terrible flirt."

"You are," Eldridge agreed.

"I'm not a *terrible* flirt, I'm an excellent flirt. And maybe I wasn't flirting. Maybe I was gathering information. You might be wrong. What if Amber didn't give Finn the drugs? What if Ed did?"

"Why do you think I'm wrong? I found a syringe in her bag for God's sake."

Then Louis said, "I didn't say I think you're wrong. I said *what if*. That's different."

"I think it's very unlikely Ed showed up here with drugs and gave them to someone he didn't know."

"Except we all knew Finn had a drug problem before we showed up. Maybe he came prepared. Maybe he wanted to get to know Finn? Did you see the prison tattoo?"

"Prison?" Well, that would explain why the tattoo was so blurry. Didn't they make them with razor blades and ballpoint pens? "Just because he was in prison, doesn't mean... Did you see Ed and Finn near each other?"

"No. Did you? Did either of you?"

I rolled my eyes, and then Ricky was standing there.

"Three eggs, lots of bacon, lots of cheese, spinach..." He looked over the other options Louis had put out, and then asked, "You have bagels?"

"We have scones."

"Yeah... What's that?"

"Like a biscuit."

"Couple of those. Dead people make me hungry."

"You're gonna have a lot of protein on your plate," Louis said, as he beat the eggs.

Like, duh, he was a body builder. I thought we were probably lucky he didn't ask to drink his omelet raw à la Rocky.

"I'm gonna slip in a workout when we break out of this place and then crash for most of the day."

Unexpectedly, Eldridge asked, "What does it feel like, knowing everyone everywhere has seen your dick?"

"Eldridge!"

"Sorry. I promised Ryan I'd ask."

"It's not that weird," Ricky said. "What *is* weird is that I had to pay so much tax on the money I made. I got taxed for showing my dick. There's something really wrong with that. I mean, it's not work."

"Yes, but… It's called income tax, not work tax," I pointed out. That earned me a dirty look.

Louis flipped Ricky's omelet onto a plate. Not as elegantly as the first one, since this one was much bigger. I handed Ricky cutlery, Eldridge gave him an evian, and then he walked away.

Then Grace was there asking, "Can you make an egg white omelet?"

"Of course. What would you like in it?"

"Nothing with fat. I struggle with my weight. Do you have any nondairy cheese?"

"No, I don't. Avocado?"

"It doesn't matter where the fat comes from. Fat is fat. And could you use something other than butter in the pan?"

"Absolutely," he said. Then he glanced at me in a way that told me I was going to have to distract her while he put butter in the pan.

"Not to be crass, but I think we all just hit a gold mine," Grace said.

"Why do you think that?" I asked, adjusting my position so she had to look away from the frying pan.

"I'm here to promote my real estate business. It was good publicity before, but now it's going to be great publicity." Squinting her eyes at me, she said, "Did someone say you have a video store? You need to make sure people know you were here. When people find out Finn overdosed while shooting this, they'll fall over themselves to watch his last appearance. There's an angle for you to work…"

"But Amber doesn't want people to know—"

"That idea is not going to work," she said.

"Because you're going to tell the truth?"

"Are you going to lie to the police?"

I was tempted to say I'd never lie to the police, but in all honesty, I had lied to the police. A lot. Which didn't mean I liked it. I answered her as best I could: "I don't know."

"Well, I'm certainly not going to lie to the police," she said. "Mainly because I can't trust the rest of you to lie. Amber can pay us, get us to sign legal agreements, threaten us, and someone will still tell the truth. That's how people work. I'm not getting caught in a lie. So I'm not going to lie... Well, I'm going to lie to Amber. That's just good business sense."

Louis was plating her omelet, which he'd somehow made look appetizing, when Wendy came back saying, "If everyone would gather around. Kathleen would like us to join her in a prayer circle."

I glanced at Louis and Eldridge, while Marc asked from the first row of the risers, "Do we have to?"

"Marc, is that your idea of a joke?" Wendy asked.

"I was going to ask *you* the same thing."

"I'm only asking for a few minutes of your time. It's not going to hurt anyone, and it will help Kathleen. She's distraught. As I'm sure you all are."

"I'm not distraught," Keely said. "I haven't seen Finn in fifteen years. He was basically a stranger."

And then Kathleen and Heston walked onto the stage. She was walking slowly, deliberately, and was very pale. Or rather, more pale. She looked like a saintly zombie.

Everyone fell silent.

Now, here's the thing about religion. If a friend was getting married in a church, I'd go. I'd sit and stand when asked, and I'd bow my head and pretend to pray. But praying with an adulterous televangelist, Kathleen True no less, who said terrible things and was likely to say something awful. Even in the space of just a few minutes. It was enough to make me sick to my stomach.

But not enough to make me actually say no.

When this was over, tomorrow morning—or rather this morning—I was going to have to call my mother. And after I gave her a moment-by-moment account of Finn's death, I would ask her what it is she did to me as a child that made me be polite to horrible people. She was always polite to horrible people, maybe that's where I learned it? But someday I wanted to unlearn it.

"If you'd all form a circle and hold hands."

Grace said, "I'm sorry, I'm going to eat my breakfast. In my dressing room." She walked off.

Ed and Ricky were basically finished with their breakfasts, so they had no excuse. We moved into the open space in front of the *Guessmate?* set.

Eldridge took my hand. There was no spark or chill up and down my spine. My heart didn't start to race. His hand wasn't overly hot or cold, it was just a normal hand attached to a cute young guy—and it felt completely right. So right that I almost pulled away.

The circle came together: Wendy and Donald flanking Kathleen; Ed, Keely and Meg came over; Ricky was eying everyone before he pushed his way between Keely and Meg, making sure there was a girl on each side of him. Marc took Meg's and Louis' hands. Louis took my other hand, while Eldridge had to hold hands with Wendy.

Notably, Heston didn't join us. Defiantly, he leaned against the stand that held the television and VCR. It was taller than he was. Kathleen stared at him a moment, obviously deciding whether to cause a scene or not. She decided not.

"Let us pray," she began. We all lowered our heads. "Dear Jesus, dear Lord above, merciful God, we call up on you to accept our dear, darling Finn into your bosom. Bring Finn home and give him a place in Heaven's village. Forgive him, Jesus. He was a sinner, like *all* of us. He fell victim to the evils of Hollywood. The drink, the drugs, the fornication, the *depravity*. We have been led astray by those claiming they're entitled to *rights*: women, Jews, homosexuals!"

Nearby, I heard Louis say under his breath, "Oh Jesus."

"Yes, yes, oh Jesus, forgive our friend. Temptation lay everywhere and he could not resist."

Honestly, it sounded canned. Like it was part of a sermon she'd done on her show. I noticed that she didn't mention his dealer. Or the people who made money importing heroin, or whatever it was that Finn overdosed on. Or a government that was more interested in putting people in prison than helping them with their addictions.

I couldn't resist raising my head slightly and looking around the circle. Everyone else dutifully had their head down. Even Louis. Then I noticed a tiny bit of movement outside the circle. Heston. I moved slightly to get a better view. He took the VCR remote out of his pocket and carefully, quietly, laid it on top of the machine.

Heston was the one responsible for the video of his mom and Finn. He must have been the one who shot it. Well, it made sense. If it happened at their house, he'd have been there.

Kathleen was still praying—or whatever. She was expanding on her theme: the evils of Hollywood, the Devil's playground. Asking God to ignore Finn's freewill and lay the entire blame at the feet of the entertainment industry—a modern day Sodom and Gomorrah. The sinful lure of fame and easy money that led Finn into the arms of Satan.

"Satan seduces with the promise of pleasure, but all he has to give is pain. The pain of being separate from God, the pain of living without God's true love—

"You know—" Meg said, stopping Kathleen cold. Kathleen gave her a death stare. Nervously, Meg continued, "I think it would be really nice if we went around the circle and said something about Finn, something we remember, something nice, something *not* about Satan."

"Satan is real. Satan is always there trying—"

"I'll go first," Keely said. "I was cast last. You'd all been rehearsing for a week. Finn was the first one to welcome me to the show. I never forgot that."

"I welcomed you to the show," Kathleen said.

"After everyone else did, and only because Wendy forced you."

"I wouldn't say *forced*," Wendy said. "That's a little extreme. Suggested, maybe."

"I remember... I always had trouble with the dance routines," Meg said. "Finn used to help me rehearse them during breaks. He didn't have to do that."

Suddenly, Finn was seeming like a much better person than I'd thought. Kathleen took a deep breath, as though she might start to pray again, so I said, "I didn't know Finn, but I really enjoyed *Sleeping With Bees*, and that romantic comedy he did, *Heartfelt*."

"Oh yes, that *was* good," Keely said.

Then Kathleen seemed to burst open, "Forgive him, Jesus! Forgive our Finn! Take him to your bosom. Take us all onto your bosom! We long to be with you. We hunger for your love, Jesus." Her face wide open, she looked up into the lights above us, and said, "There! There it is! The golden light of Jesus."

Okay, I couldn't help but look. You know, just in case. And what I saw was absolutely nothing out of the ordinary. Just lights. Well, not just lights. There was a bit of movement, and I caught a glimpse of Amber on the catwalk. What was she doing up there?

"Jesus! Jesus, I see you! Our savior! Come to me. Come to me, Jesus!"

I looked back to Kathleen; her face was enrapt. She said in a trembling voice, "We are blessed! We are the chosen!"

And then she threw up.

FIFTEEN

Yeah, so that was disgusting. People were moving in every direction, mostly away from Kathleen, saying things like, "Oh God" and "Yuck."

Wendy immediately called out, "Louis! Can you clean this up?!"

"Um, I was hired to put food in... Not deal with it when it comes out."

After she wiped her mouth, Kathleen began to scream, "What's happening to me?!"

"Ed, would you..." Wendy said. The grip walked by them to go to the craft room and get wet paper towels.

Donald was saying, "Kathleen, Kathleen... it's going to be all right."

"What the fuck do you know about it?" she snarled at him, suddenly falling completely out of character. Making me wonder, briefly, what it must be like to spend your whole life playing a part. All the time. Each and every day. Then she slipped back into character. "Jesus! Jesus, take me home!"

Wendy and Donald led her back to her dressing room. I wondered where Heston had gone to. He hadn't participated in the prayer circle, which was weird. I mean, he didn't look like he was following his mother's path, but she did seem like the type to insist that he at least pray.

"Is it possible Finn didn't overdose?" Eldridge asked.

"What makes you say—"

"I mean, she sort of has some of the same symptoms. He got kind of delusional, and she just got... kind of delusional. Unless you really think she saw Jesus?"

"I seriously doubt she saw Jesus," Louis said. "Even if I believed it possible to see Jesus, I doubt a vision of our Lord and Savior would be followed by vomiting."

"It was Amber on the catwalk," I said.

"What was she doing up there?" Marc asked.

"She wanted to make calls," I said. "Maybe there's a signal up there. Or maybe she's trying to find a way onto the roof."

"If she got on the roof there'd be a signal. Do you think she'd have the decency to call the police?" Louis asked.

Marc, Eldridge and I said "No" at the same time.

"Do you think Kathleen's going to die?" I asked.

"I hope not," Eldridge said. "I mean, not because I like her. I just—"

"You guys don't think Finn was on drugs? You think they were both poisoned?" I asked them both.

"I do," Louis said. "The thing is... they didn't have anything other than the Juicy Juices, did they?"

"Neither of them came to the table while I was there," Eldridge said. "And pretty much everyone else ate from the table at some point."

"They each had a pop," I remembered. "Amber brought Finn a Diet Coke. I didn't see him drink it, though. Later I brought a 7-Up, but that was after he got sick. Kathleen had a 7-Up. We're talking cans, though. It would be very difficult to put anything in them. And, well, no one could know who'd get which can."

"There had to have been something in the Juicy Juice."

"But everyone had a Juicy Juice," I pointed out.

"It has to be in the special green goop they use. Both drinks used that. And no one else had it." Louis looked at me closely, then very calmly said, "We should go get that and keep it safe."

The three of us hurried back to the craft room. Marc and the others had already gone back to their dressing rooms. Once we were in the craft room, Louis opened the cooler that contained all the fruit. Very quickly he saw... "It's not here."

"Someone got here first," I said, stating the obvious.

"What do you think they'll do with it?" Eldridge asked.

"They'll want to find a way to get rid of it," Louis said. He glanced at the sink, which was still filled with ice and sodas. "Obviously, they didn't get rid of it in here."

"Bathroom," I said. "I'd flush it down the toilet."

We dashed out of the craft room and down the hall to the restrooms. When we entered the men's room, I was surprised by how small it was. There was only a toilet and a sink. There was no window. When I turned on the light a fan built into the ceiling came on.

"What are we looking for, exactly?" Eldridge asked.

Louis was looking into the toilet, and he said, "This."

I stepped over and looked down. There were two cigarette butts floating in the toilet. It was disgusting, but it did make sense. Southern California was constantly going in and out of droughts. We'd all learned long ago that you didn't flush a toilet unless absolutely necessary. Cigarette butts would not count as a necessary flush.

"So, the green goop wasn't flushed down this toilet," I said.

"Nope."

Without a word, Louis left the men's room and ran into the women's room next to it. Eldridge and I were right behind him.

"I beg your pardon!" Grace said when we entered.

She was leaning up against the wall smoking a cigarette. It was very crowded in there with the four of us.

"I could have been using the facilities!"

"Then you'd have locked the door," Louis said. He stepped over and stared into the toilet.

"This is all too weird. I needed a cigarette."

"You didn't flush the toilet, did you?" Louis asked.

"No. I told you. I came in here to smoke."

"Was anyone in here?"

"No. What's going on?"

"We think Kathleen and Finn were poisoned," I explained. "And the poison was in the green goop they use for some of the drinks. Now the green goop is missing."

Of course, I realized immediately that Grace could have been the poisoner, and she'd just come down here to flush the evidence down the toilet and cover up by smoking—no, I didn't think it was her. When would she have poisoned the goop? How would she even know there would be goop? And how would she know who'd be drinking the goop?

"Let me get this straight. Someone poisoned the drinks. So why isn't he the main suspect?" She pointed at Louis.

"Because he's the one who figured it out," Eldridge said.

"It wouldn't be the first time a killer pretended to solve the crime in their favor."

"He also has no reason to poison Finn and Kathleen," I pointed out.

"They were both annoying. Isn't that a good enough reason?"

Louis looked at Eldridge and I as he said, "Let's go find Marc." We were about to walk out of the women's room, when Grace said, "You know, there are restrooms in the big dressing rooms. Someone could have flushed the goop down one of those toilets."

"Thanks," I said.

The Zola Emery dressing room was only a few feet away. We stood outside the door, hesitating. There was still a dead body on the other side of the door, after all. Louis took a deep breath, and said, "Let's get this over with."

We opened the door, and there was Finn still on the sofa, still without his pants. Amber and Ricky stood on the other side of the room whispering to each other. They stopped abruptly, and Amber asked, "What do you want?"

"We don't think Finn overdosed. We think he was poisoned," I said.

I watched her reaction closely. She was guarded, seeming to make quick calculations about how that information fit into her plans. Was she relieved Finn didn't die of an overdose? It was hard to tell.

"Why do you think that?"

"Because Finn and Kathleen had the same symptoms: vomiting, confusion, disconnecting from reality."

She smirked, "So you don't think she actually saw Jesus?"

"No, I don't," I said. "What she saw was you up on the catwalk trying to make a call. Did you get any bars?"

Ignoring my question, she asked, "What do you think they were poisoned with?"

"The only thing Finn and Kathleen ate or drank was the Juicy Juice I made for them," Louis said. "They both had a drink made with the special green goop I was provided. We think that's where the poison was. The goop has disappeared and we're checking to see if someone flushed it down the toilet."

"How long have you been in here?" I asked.

"We just came in here a couple of minutes ago," Amber said. There was a flush in her cheeks. I didn't ask why they were in there; I was pretty sure I knew, and they didn't volunteer the information.

Louis went into the bathroom. Eldridge and I followed him. It was another cramped little room. Even if they wanted to, Amber and Ricky couldn't have followed us. Shoulder to shoulder, the three of us stared into the toilet.

"Look," Louis said very quietly.

On one side of the bowl was a small green smudge. Louis leaned over, took a piece of toilet paper and wiped up the smudge. He folded it over and put it into his jeans pocket.

"Well, did you find what you were looking for?" Amber asked.

"No," Louis lied. "Someone could have flushed the goop down but there's no sign of it."

"Are you seriously telling me that Finn didn't overdose?"

"Yes. Finn didn't overdose," Louis said.

I could see where she might be confused. I'd found a syringe in her bag. Did she give him a dose of heroin and *then* he was poisoned by the drink? Is that what happened? Or was there something else going on? And what would that something be?

"What time is it?" she asked.

"Almost four," Louis said. And that explained why my eyes felt like they were filled with sand.

"So, I've got three hours to turn this mess around."

How she was going to do that, I had no idea. And what exactly did she mean? She wouldn't be bringing Finn back from the dead. And as long as he was dead it would be a mess.

"Do you think someone poisoned Finn and Kathleen specifically?" she asked.

"They'd have to have known what they were going to drink," Louis said.

"Wendy has a list," Ricky said. "She wanted to give me some pineapple drink. I asked for the Banana Blast because it has potassium. Wait... Do you think I'd have been poisoned too if I'd had the drink she wanted me to have?"

"No," Louis said. "The Pineapple Punch doesn't have any green goop in it."

"It does sound like whoever did this had access to the list," Eldridge said. "That's how they'd know Finn and Kathleen were having drinks with the green stuff."

"Not Kathleen," I said. "She specifically asked for a Green Goddess when she was supposed to have a Blue Moon."

Louis said, "I had a copy of the list. Wendy emailed it to me at work. I printed it out and brought it, but it disappeared before I had time to make any drinks."

"Were you the only one to get the email?"

"No. There were CCs. I didn't pay attention, though, so I don't remember who got the email. I can print it out when I get to work on Monday, but that doesn't help right now."

"So, some people got the list by email. But yours disappeared, so anyone could have taken it from you and figured out who was going to drink what. How long was it before you noticed the list was missing?"

"I made Finn's drink about a half an hour or so after we got here. The list was already gone."

"And you'd been running back and forth between the stage and the craft room?"

He nodded. "Anyone could have taken it."

"None of that is good," Amber said. "If Finn was murdered, then he should be the *only* victim. There can't be an accidental victim or a second victim. That doesn't make a good story. Wait... Maybe it's a better story if someone were trying to kill Finn *and* Kathleen. Someone jealous. Meg knows about plants. Maybe she had a thing for Finn. Maybe she put some poisonous plant into the goop. It would really be helpful if Meg killed them both."

"Um, Kathleen's not dead," I said.

"But she could be. Any minute. Right?"

We just shrugged since we had no idea. It really seemed like Amber was hoping Kathleen would die. I glanced at Louis. We'd both had enough of this. He said, "Let's go find Marc."

We stepped out into the hallway. At the far end, we could see that people were gathered outside Kathleen's dressing room. Before we walked down, Louis said, "I need to wash my hands real quick. I'll meet you down there."

It made sense. He had just had his hands in a toilet. He popped into the men's room, leaving me with Eldridge. As we walked down the hallway, he said quietly, "You didn't say anything about the syringe you found. Why not?"

"I don't know. I don't know what she's up to, so it seemed like a good idea to stay quiet."

Eldridge nodded, like that was a great strategic move—it probably wasn't. Then he said, "Something was going on there, wasn't it? Between Amber and Ricky, I mean. Do you think they're doing it?"

"No," I said. "Ricky was looking for a phone earlier. Said he wanted to call his girlfriend at two in the morning. I think he was going to call the tabloids about Finn's overdose."

"So, you think he was trying to blackmail Amber for more money?"

"Yeah, that's what I think."

"What if it's him? What if he poisoned Finn so he could sell the story to the tabloids?"

"Hmmm... That would be very entrepreneurial, I suppose."

And then we reached Marc, Keely and Meg outside of Kathleen's dressing room. The door to the dressing room was shut. I asked, "Do you know what's going on in there?"

"She's still alive," Marc said. "We keep hearing groans."

"Who's in there with her?" Eldridge asked.

"The producers and Heston."

A moment later, Louis joined us.

"Did you tell them?" he asked.

"Not yet."

"Tell us what?" Marc wanted to know.

"Their drinks were poisoned. Finn and Kathleen each had a green-based drink. There was something in the green goop."

"Really?" Meg said. "Oh my God!"

In a low voice, Keely said, "It's that kid. Heston. He did it."

"Why do you say that?" I asked.

"You saw his eyes. Finn is obviously his father. I mean, I'd kill Kathleen if she was my mom. And I'd kill Finn for leaving me with her."

As if to remind us she was still alive, we heard Kathleen moan through the door.

"But he's just a kid. What is he, fourteen?"

"Kids are scary," Keely said. "Believe me, I know."

"Because you're Black?" Meg asked.

Keely rolled her eyes. "Because I was in a production of *The Bad Seed*. That's what got me onto *Kapowie!*"

"Oh, sorry."

"There's that woman back East who had a bunch of teenage boys kill her husband," Marc said.

"Oh, they're making a movie out of that," Eldridge said.

"They are?" I asked.

"Don't you read *Variety*?"

I didn't. The subscription was way too expensive.

"It can't be Heston," I said. "Kathleen wasn't supposed to have a green drink. Unless he was trying to kill Finn and only accidentally poisoned his mother."

"What if she dies?" Meg said, her voice nearly a wail. "And all we've done is stand here."

"We're trapped in here," Marc said. "There's nothing we can do about it."

"Wait, I think there might be," I said, then asked Marc, "Do you remember what Donald said when we asked about an emergency?"

"There's a fire alarm," he said. "Do you remember where it is?"

I thought back to Marc, Grace, and me going from door to door checking to see if they were all jammed shut. Where was the fire alarm? Was there just one? We started with the door we came through and then worked our way around the building from corner to corner.

"It's near the door we came in through," I said.

"Let's go pull it."

We were practically there. We opened the door that led to the exit door. There was the fire alarm about five feet up from the floor next to the door. I reached out and pulled the lever.

And nothing happened.

SIXTEEN

Nothing at all. There was no ear-splitting alarm. No flashing lights. No guard rushing over to the door to open it. There was only silence. Well, not silence; there was still the occasional moan coming from Kathleen's dressing room.

"Do you think it goes off at the guard station?" Eldridge asked. "Do you think it's supposed to be silent?"

"No, I think the point of a fire alarm is to get people to exit the building. That's why it's by the exit, so that you can pull it on your way out."

I waited for panic and dread to overtake me. I mean, it should, right? We were trapped in this building and there had been a murder, with possibly a second in progress. I was exactly where I didn't want to be. And yet, I knew I only had to get through a few more hours and the doors would be opened, and the murder or murders would be a police matter.

"We're really trapped in here," Marc said. "That's creepy. It's like we're in a slasher movie."

"Sweetheart," Louis said, "No one's been stabbed."

"I meant metaphorically."

"This has to be deliberate," I said, far more clear-headed than I should have been.

"You think it was all planned?" Louis asked.

"The doors are jammed, the phone doesn't work, there's no key for the elephant door, and the fire alarm doesn't go off," I said. "It couldn't *all* be coincidental."

I studied the fire alarm, which was attached to a metal conduit that rose nearly forty feet to the ceiling. Somewhere the alarm had been disconnected, either in the alarm box itself or up on the ceiling. It can't have been easy or fast.

"Someone put a lot of thought into keeping us in here."

"That would have to be Donald," Marc said. "He's already admitted to having the doors jammed."

"Other people knew about that though," I said. "Wendy must have known. Ed might have. The guard knew, definitely. There were negotiations with Amber Bright and Kathleen's people. Donald probably didn't tell them we were being trapped inside, but we don't know he didn't. Not to mention, we know Alan, the guard, takes bribes. Any one of us could have come by last night or the night before and bribed him to let us have a look around. At that point, the phone line could have been cut and the fire alarm disconnected. I don't think we can narrow things down quite yet."

"Well, *I* didn't do it," Keely said.

"Me neither," Meg said.

I was about to say, 'No offense, but I'm not taking your word for it,' when Eldridge said, "It would help if we knew what kind of poison we were talking about."

"Well... we know it was in the green goop," I said.

"Which is what, exactly?"

"It's proprietary, but Louis thinks it's..."

He took over for me, "Spinach, kale and other greens."

If my life was a movie, this is where there'd have been a shot of fireworks going off. I'd have had an epiphany, which might have to do with the fact that I was standing with a botanist *and* a florist. "It would be really easy to mix in some kind of poison plant."

"You're right, it would be," Louis said.

"You're saying it's one of us? You think Keely or I poisoned them? I have absolutely no motive," Meg said.

"Except two years of being called the fat chick," Marc pointed out. "I'm sorry, but that is what they called you."

"I remember. They called me that to my face. But that was fifteen years ago. I've had a long time to get over it. And I'm comfortable with myself now. I've found a particular kind of gentleman who like a bit of booty."

"Oh my God, you like Black guys," Keely said.

"I have been known to date a brother or two."

"Please don't say it that way."

"What?"

"It's just wrong."

"What's wrong?"

"Forget it."

Clearly, Meg didn't understand. She gathered herself, and said, "So you see I have no motive. Besides, it doesn't take a degree in botany to know some plants are poisonous. Many of them are. Most will just make you sick. Very few of them will kill you. Not in the amounts we're talking about."

"You're trying to say it's me, aren't you?" Keely said to Meg.

"I didn't say—"

"You noticed the flowers right away. You made a point of telling me they're poisonous even though I told you I knew that."

"Calm down," Meg said. "Anyone can find out that foxglove is poisonous. Anyone could have added some of that or another plant to the… green goop Louis keeps talking about."

"So, it's a coincidence that foxglove is in the floral arrangements Keely brought?" I asked.

"Of course it's a coincidence," Keely said. "Look, they're tall and beautiful, and they give a display structure. And you need structure. You don't want to just have short little balls of flowers. I mean, yes, some florists sell those flowers in a bowl, but, personally, I hate those."

"Were you asked to bring those arrangements?" Louis wanted to know.

"Yes, of course. They paid me two hundred and fifty dollars."

"Who ordered the flowers?"

"Donald and Wendy."

"Both of them?"

"I think so. I got emails from each of them."

"Did they specifically ask for foxglove?" I asked.

She frowned. "They both asked for the tall, spiky flower with trumpets. I don't think they knew the name. They just described what they wanted. Wait—do you think they wanted to make it seem like I poisoned Finn and Kathleen? So no one would figure out it was them?"

"We don't know what's going on," I said. "That's why we're asking questions."

"Why would they want to poison Finn and Kathleen?" Marc asked. "Donald seems really happy this is happening. Or was. Now that Finn is dead, who knows if this will get on the air."

"Wendy is not as excited, though," Eldridge pointed out. "She seems more interested in the juice business."

"You're right," I said. "But I don't think she'd use her juice to poison Finn and Kathleen, even if she did want them dead."

Then I heard Wendy's voice, "Hello!? Where did everyone go? Louis!"

"Oh God," he said, next to me.

"Right here, Wendy," he said as he opened the door to the hallway. We trailed in behind him. Wendy was standing there in the doorway of the Arbuckle dressing room.

"Oh good. Can you get us some cans of 7-Up? We need to try and keep Kathleen hydrated. And does anyone have Pepto Bismol or Tums or anything like that?"

Louis walked down the hallway as Meg said, "I have some Pepto." She and Keely walked out to the stage to get it from Meg's purse.

When they were gone, Marc asked me, "What do you think? Do you think Meg or Keely is behind this?"

"You know them better than I do."

"I knew them fifteen years ago. People can change a lot in fifteen years. Look at me for instance."

"Keely knew who you were," I said.

"Did she? I mean, she was only a few feet away when Wendy thought you were me. Maybe she heard the whole thing."

"Oh wow, I guess you're right."

"You're saying we have no idea if either of them could have done it," Eldridge said.

"They *probably* didn't do anything. But I wouldn't completely cross them off the list." The list that was stubbornly not getting shorter.

"Who do you think is most likely to have poisoned Finn and Kathleen?" Eldridge asked Marc.

"They both got preferential treatment and probably more money. I think Ricky resents that more than the rest of us."

"So he's got a motive," I said.

"Maybe."

"But do you think he planned it all before he got here? Did he bring poison with him? Did he run around cutting phone lines and fire alarms?"

"Maybe."

I tried to think it through. Could it have been Ricky? He had a mobile phone with him but couldn't get it to work. That's why he wanted to use the office phone. But, well, he could have been the one to cut the cord and just pretended he wanted to use the phone. Did he already know the doors were jammed? I wasn't sure if he'd been around while we were talking about it, but then… he could have tried going outside to use his mobile and found out on his own.

What about the poison? There were lots of opportunities to get to the green goop. He could easily have gotten to Finn's drink since it was on ice for a long time before Louis gave it to Finn.

Did he bring the poison with him? Or did he somehow get ahold of some of the foxglove from one of the displays? Should we have Keely check the displays for missing flowers? Would it have been enough, though? No, Ricky was starting to feel implausible. There were too many could have's but not enough did's.

The door to the dressing room opened again, and Wendy said, "Do you mind? We can hear you talking." Then Louis was there with the 7-Up. Wendy grabbed it without a thank-you.

We moved down to the craft room, and Marc said, "What if it's her?"

"You mean Wendy?" I asked.

"What are you talking about?" Louis said.

"We were talking about who might have poisoned Finn and Kathleen," Marc said.

"Right outside Kathleen's dressing room?"

"Maybe not such a great idea," I said.

Louis shook his head and said, "I'm going to go check the table. What time is it?"

"Almost four thirty," Marc said.

"We're going to start packing up in about an hour or so. I'll do a last call kind of thing around ten of six, maybe?"

We nodded. What did we know about catering? Particularly catering during a murder. Louis rolled his eyes at us and walked away. I asked, "Marc, do you really think it could be Wendy?"

Marc shrugged. "She could be in there destroying evidence."

"Or she could just be kind," Eldridge suggested. "I mean, *someone* should be concerned that Kathleen is sick."

"It's kind of hard to care," I said. "She's spent a lot of time saying horrible things about people with AIDS."

"Where's Grace?" Marc asked. "I haven't seen her in a while."

"She was smoking in the ladies' room last time I saw her. She thinks Louis poisoned Finn and Kathleen because they're annoying."

"Why would she accuse Louis?" Marc asked sharply.

"I don't think she was serious."

"And you just *let* her say that?"

"Louis was right there. He's a grown—"

"She said it *to* him?! And I thought she was my friend."

"You haven't seen her in fifteen years."

"Yeah, well, we smoked together. It's a bond."

With that, he started stomping down the hallway. I hurried after him with Eldridge in tow. "Marc. Take a breath."

"I will not take a breath. This is no time for breathing."

I looked over my shoulder at Eldridge, and said, "Oh God."

Moments later we crashed through the door to the ladies' room. Grace was still inside; she had a cigarette in one hand and what looked like a wad of toilet paper in the other. Her eyes were swollen and bright pink. She'd clearly been crying. Actually, she still was crying. I was bracing myself to listen to Marc yell at a crying woman, when I heard him say, "Oh honey, what's wrong?"

"I shouldn't have come. I thought I could deal with this, but I can't. Did you find a way out? I can't stay here. I have to leave. I have to—"

"Why Grace? What is it you need to get away from?"

Very quietly she said, "Heston."

"Oh, I see," Marc said. "Look we've all figured out that Finn was his dad, and that Kathleen didn't actually adopt him. That's she's really his mother."

"She's not his mother."

"She's not?"

"No. I am."

SEVENTEEN

Grace held out the wad of toilet paper that was not toilet paper at all but was instead a Polaroid photo. Marc took it and unfolded it. Next to him, I could see that it was a photo of a very young Grace. She was wearing a smock-style blouse that covered the top of her jeans. She was making a face at the camera.

"After Marc found the cigarette case, I wondered if there was anything for me. I started looking around. It was in the drawer... makeup table... on my side. Not hard to find. I remember that top. I started wearing it when I couldn't button the top button on my jeans."

"What happened, Grace?" Marc asked. "How did you—"

"It was stupid. A one-night thing with Finn and I was pregnant. That's all. I was still a kid, barely eighteen. Wes drove me to get it taken care of, but when we got there I couldn't go through with it. He was so sweet about it. I was hoping he'd be here tonight. I've always wanted to know what happened to him. I owe him."

Marc lit a cigarette, then asked, "Gracie, why does Kathleen have your son? Did she kidnap him?"

Shaking her head, she started slowly, "It's funny how murky things can get years later. Especially when things are... hard. I know Kathleen and Finn broke up around the time the show ended. I think it was about Finn's night with me, though no one's ever said so directly. I had the baby the following fall. That first year with Heston, I couldn't cope. I had a little money from a trust fund, the money I'd made acting as a kid. But it wasn't enough to hire help. And my parents... There was no one. I was stuck there with him all the time. Alone. I couldn't go to auditions. I couldn't get work. I was struggling. No one was helping me. Meanwhile, Kathleen had married Winthrop True. He wasn't as famous then. It didn't seem... Anyway, that's when Kathleen found out her uterus is about as hospitable as the Mojave Desert. She wanted to adopt, so she came to me."

"Why didn't she take a more traditional route?" I asked. "Going to an old friend isn't the usual route to adopt a child."

"I suspect following the traditional route would have exposed some skeletons in their closets. I mean, they're con artists. I *think* her husband even has a criminal record to that effect. A few years ago, I helped them buy a house in Newport Beach. They tried getting a traditional mortgage, but the broker started asking a lot of questions about Winthrop. Eventually, they had their church buy the house for them. Of course, that was much later. When we did the adoption I didn't ask a lot of questions. Honestly, I was just grateful. Their lawyer arranged everything. There was money involved, which I used to get my real estate license and put a down payment on my first condo."

I resisted the temptation to point out she'd sold her child. Instead, I asked, "Are you sorry?"

"I like who I am. I like the things I have. It would have been nice to get here another way, but that's not what happened."

I believed her, even as she wiped tears off her cheeks.

"Why did you come tonight?"

She took a deep breath to calm herself. "I never thought she'd bring him. I thought it unlikely we'd even talk about him. Silly me."

"And Finn?"

"Finn? Finn's a little boy. Was. For all the talk of men running the world it's interesting how often they end up being completely insignificant."

That took me aback. They'd had sex and she was the one who'd paid a price. But then, well, she was also the one who made all the decisions. She and Kathleen. It didn't sound like they'd considered Finn at all.

Then I wondered if she was lying. Finn was responsible for her having a child. Kathleen took that child away. It's not a stretch to think she might be angry about at least some of what happened. She could be trying to cover that up.

"I didn't poison Finn, if that's what you're thinking," she said, wiping more tears. "I told you already, I've made quite a bit of money buying and selling houses for him. Not to mention the referrals I've gotten from him. Killing him would be shooting myself in the foot."

That all sounded very rational—something I'd learned murderers often weren't. I glanced at Marc; he was eating it up with a spoon.

"You poor thing. And here I thought you were just a rich bitch."

"No, I'm just a rich bitch with a past. As most of us are." A weak smile crossed her tear-stained face before she said, "Please don't tell Heston. He doesn't deserve any of this."

"Of course not," I said. Eldridge and Marc chimed in with similar comments.

When Eldridge and I got back to the stage—Marc stayed with Grace to have another cigarette—we stood near the table with Louis. Donald was behind the camera again. They'd set up in front of the blue curtain and Wendy was sitting on the stool.

"Can you believe this?" Louis asked.

I couldn't. How could they continue? Two people had been poisoned and one of them was dead. Even if OTN still wanted the show, the police would be taking the tapes as evidence, wouldn't they? They'd be lucky to ever get them back. None of that seemed to have occurred to Donald, who'd just gotten the camera positioned the way he wanted it. "Are you ready, sweetheart?"

Notably, Wendy was not holding a Juicy Juice. I was sure that meant something, but I wasn't sure what. Did she want to downplay the juice since it likely figured in Finn's death and Kathleen's illness? Did she even realize that? We hadn't told her. Or did she have a more realistic idea about the fate of the reunion show?

Donald said action and Wendy began.

"Donald and I met when we were theater students at a small Christian college in western Kentucky. After we graduated, we came to Hollywood and supported ourselves by producing and directing musicals at a summer camp in Oxnard, caroling during the holidays, and anything else we could think of to pay the rent. In the mid-seventies, we produced a sort of variety show for teenagers, *Stars of Tomorrow*, on the Westside. It was actually a really smart idea. You put eight or nine teenagers into a show, and you're guaranteed that at least two or even three hundred friends and family will show up to see them. And, of course, there was a participation fee. It was actually lucrative. We started getting write-ups in the smaller newspapers and then, suddenly, we were in talks to turn it all into a television show for Saturday mornings."

"What are your fondest memories of *Kapowie!*, Wendy?"

"I'd have to say working with you, Donald. I think it was the best period of our marriage. We had so much hope for the future. We thought we were going places. We were so in love then."

"Cut," Donald said, turning off the camera. "Wendy that might be a little too personal."

He didn't seem at all bothered by what she'd just said. We were so in love *then* implies they're not so in love now. That went over his head, entirely.

Wendy said, "Of course. I'll give it another try."

He pressed the button. "Action." After leaving a beat he asked, "What are your fondest memories of *Kapowie!*?"

"I'd have to say the kids. They were so fresh-faced, so excited to be there—"

"Cut," Donald said. Wendy gave him a disgruntled look. "Wendy, you know I'm planning on talking about the kids. We shouldn't talk about the same thing."

"If I can't talk about you and I can't talk about the kids, what am I allowed to talk about?"

"The music, the dancing, the skits, the educational merit."

"All right, fine," she said tersely.

She steamed as he put his finger on the button and said, "Action."

For the third time he asked, "What are your fondest memories of *Kapowie!*?"

She left a long pause before she said, "The thing I'm most proud of is teaching kids not to take drugs, not to drink or smoke, to hold off on sex until they were older, not to give in to peer pressure, to respect themselves and allow themselves to be children as long as they could be."

Then she took another moment before continuing, "And I'm proud of the fact that we did all that with songs and jokes and dance numbers. We didn't lecture, we didn't talk down to the kids. We tried to be on their level and teach them good lessons."

After a beat, Donald said, "Wendy that was great. Now could you do an intro for the dance number?"

"We're not still going to do that, are we? I mean, after the things that have happened. Even if they do go on with the reunion show, they're not going to want video of the cast dancing without Finn and Kathleen. It's creepy, Donald. And in bad taste."

"We should have it just to have it though. Just in case." I took that to mean he'd put it in whether it was creepy or not.

"It sounds like you *want* to film the cast doing the dance number. I don't think you should. And I don't think you *can*. I don't think they'll cooperate."

"I'd like to try.

"If you manage to film it, I can introduce it over footage from the show. You don't need it now."

"But..." Donald took a moment and then gave up. "Is there anything else you'd like to talk about?"

"No, I'm fine."

"You wouldn't like to say a few words about Juicy Juice?"

"Why don't you do it, Donald. You talk about the stores."

"The stores are yours."

"The stores are *ours*." Then she looked around, saying, "Louis... Where's Louis?"

"Here."

"Donald would like a Hawaiian Sunset. Could you make him one?"

"I'd rather have a Giant Green Monster," Donald said. "That's my favorite."

"Oh no," Wendy said. "You know it gives you gas. I'm not— no, just no."

"Hawaiian Sunset it is," Louis said. Louis gave me a look as he left.

That little exchange might mean a lot. Or maybe it meant nothing. Did she know the green goop had been poisoned? We hadn't told them. More importantly, was it safe to make drinks that didn't have the green goop? Well... probably. The green goop had disappeared, meaning whoever poisoned it didn't want to get caught. Yes, they could have poisoned some of the other ingredients. But why would they? And then I had the thought, *It wasn't random.* Whoever was behind this had meant to poison Finn. They weren't trying to kill us all. I have to say I relaxed a bit. Well, a tiny bit.

Wendy got off the stool and came away from the set. Donald and Ed moved the camera to the yellow curtain in the middle of the set.

I leaned in close to Eldridge and asked, "How are you doing?"

"I'm very tired, but I'm too busy being freaked out to really notice. I can't believe everything that's happened in one night."

"I'm sorry about all this. I shouldn't have gotten you involved."

"Don't be stupid. You had no idea it would turn out like this."

That was a debatable point. Things seemed to turn out like this a lot. I had the feeling we weren't likely to get paid. If they didn't pay us, I should really pay him. Just pretend he worked at Pinx for the night. Of course, that got me wondering, "You know… none of my business but I don't pay you enough to live on. How do you survive?"

"Scholarships, student loans, I have two roommates and my aunt pays half my rent."

"And your parents?"

"Yeah… I have parents."

Ouch. That was not a warm and cozy response. I decided it was best left alone.

"Mikey says your mom is really sweet."

"She is. She's also *my* mom, so she can be… trying."

Oh God, I shouldn't have said that since his parents were obviously much more trying than my mother could ever be. I mean, it was true, she could get on my nerves. But I was obviously much better off than he was. His parents didn't seem to be helping him through college, while my mother just bought me a used car—and the only reason it was used is that I wouldn't let her buy me a new one. Eldridge was smirking at me, which made me feel like he was reading my mind.

"What?"

"You're cute. That's all."

Before I could remind him that we would not be going on any dates, Wendy called out, "Quiet! We're going to film again."

Once the stage was quiet, she said, "Are you ready, Donald?"

"Yes."

"Action."

There was a short beat before Donald said, "You have to press the button."

"I told you Ed should do this," Wendy said, then pressed the button. "Action."

Beat.

"Well, I have exciting news," Donald began. "OTN has just agreed to bring *Kapowie!* back. The show will feature songs, dance, jokes, skits... all with strong family values. We'll be conducting a nationwide search for eight new teenage stars to make twenty new episodes. Well, seven new teenage stars. We've already chosen the first cast member. Original cast member Kathleen's son... Heston True!"

There was a beat before Wendy said, "Cut! Donald, you didn't tell me Heston was going to be in the new show."

"Kathleen confirmed it this afternoon."

"Can he do anything? Can he sing or dance or tell jokes?"

"We'll have to find out."

"You don't know? You didn't audition him? Did you even ask if he had any talent?"

"Of course, I didn't ask. They want him on the show. Kathleen wants him on the show. That's the reason it's getting made. That's the reason you and I are going to be in the industry again."

"Why is that so damned important, Donald? We're fine. We have everything we need. We don't *need* this. We don't need *any* of this."

"I need this. I don't want to sell smoothies for the rest of my life. I want a voice. I want to be heard. Can't you understand that? Can't you of all people—"

She stepped forward and put her arms around him. They stayed like that for a long moment.

Meanwhile, I debated whether a kid's show like *Kapowie!* really had a 'voice'. I mean, it was pretty awful. And it seemed like other people were telling him what it was going to be. But I guess having a voice didn't necessarily mean you got to say whatever you wanted or had something important to say or that you could say it well. After a long moment they separated, and Donald said,

"Can we finish this now? I'd like to talk about our NATTY. Could you get it out of my bag, dear?"

Most people don't know this, but a NATTY is the National Award for Teenage Television. It was a very low-level award that never really caught on. They stopped giving them out in the eighties.

Wendy went over to Donald's camera bag and zipped it open. She quickly found the NATTY and was about to close up the bag, but then stopped. After staring into the bag for a long moment, she pulled out a prescription bottle.

"Donald? Why is my medicine in your bag?"

"I don't know. Did you put it there?"

"Why would you ask that? If I put it there I wouldn't be surprised to find it there now, would I?"

"Well, I didn't put it there. Why would I put it there?"

"Maybe you didn't want me taking my meds tonight."

"That's ridiculous. Why would I want you to *not* take your meds. If anything, I'd want you *to* take your meds. You're always very annoying when you don't take your meds."

"What is that supposed to mean?"

"Oh, for God's sake, Wendy, just take your pill so we can get on with this."

She popped open the prescription bottle. Reaching one finger into the vial, she stopped, then took her finger out so she could look down into the orange bottle.

"Donald, half my pills are gone."

"Did you knock the bottle over somewhere?"

"I didn't knock the bottle over and I didn't put the bottle in your bag."

"Well, I don't know what happened. You know you forget things."

"I haven't forgotten that I forget," she said angrily. Then she stormed over to him, shoved the NATTY into his arms, and thumped over to the craft table. She grabbed an evian and took her pill. Immediately afterward, she shoved some shortbread into her mouth.

"Ed, can you operate the camera?" Donald asked. He seemed relatively unperturbed.

"Sure thing." Ed got behind the camera, then asked, "Are you ready?"

"Yes, I am."

"All right then. Action."

Donald barely left the beat he'd been telling everyone else to leave. "In nineteen seventy-eight at the end of our first season, we were lucky enough to win a NATTY award for excellence in teenage television."

He held the award up to camera. There was a rustling sound behind us, and I turned to see that Kathleen was standing just inside the sound stage. The heels and the wig were gone, so she was much smaller. She was barely taller than her son, who was holding her up. Her hair was cut into a mousy pixie.

"Where is he?" she croaked. "Where is the son of a bitch who poisoned me?"

EIGHTEEN

"Louis!" Wendy screamed out. "We need you out here!"

And at that exact moment Louis came onto the stage holding the Hawaiian Sunset he'd made for Donald. Behind him were Marc, Keely and Meg. They'd obviously been gossiping, but Louis covered by saying, "Sorry that took so long. We're almost out of pineapple. Just an FYI."

Dead silence. Everyone was staring at him. He noticed and asked, "What?"

"You!" Kathleen hissed. "You poisoned me."

"Not on purpose."

"I don't believe you. You killed Finn! And you were trying to kill me!"

"Kathleen, you've been through a lot. It's been a very challenging night for you, but no one's been poisoned..." Wendy said. "You're confused."

"It was in *your* drink."

"What? No, that's not possible. Our drinks are healthy."

"It was in the green goop," Louis explained.

"Green goo—the proprietary green blend, you mean."

"Whoever poisoned it stole the rest of it and flushed it down the toilet."

"No. That's simply not—"

Donald said, "Louis, you have a lot to answer for."

"Me? You're the one who gave me the ingredients."

"There's nothing in my juices except healthy fruits, various additives and secret ingredients," Wendy yelled.

"Calm down," I said. "Just because there was something in the drinks it doesn't mean *you* put it there. And just because Louis made the drinks doesn't mean he put poison in them either."

"You're just trying to cover for your friend!" Kathleen said.

"Why would I poison you or Finn Henderson?" Louis asked.

"Jealousy. You're jealous of normal people, people like Finn and me."

I felt she was kind stretching it to call a rabidly homophobic televangelist and a drug-addicted movie star normal. If anyone was normal it was Marc and Louis, two guys with boring jobs who loved each other. And, you know, occasionally solved murders. Okay, maybe that last part wasn't normal.

Louis said, "I don't know either of you, and believe me, I'm not jealous of you."

"Marc. Marc made you do it," she said. "He hates—"

"First of all, Marc doesn't *make* me do anything. And—"

"You're sick degenerates who'd do just about anything to ruin the lives—"

"Kathleen, that's enough," Heston said.

"Call me Mom!"

"Sure, MOM! Why don't you ever remember the nice parts of the Bible? You know, the parts about being *nice*."

"Are you saying I'm *not* nice?"

"That's exactly what I'm saying!"

The fact that she appeared to be shocked by that was in itself shocking. She'd probably heard before that she wasn't very nice, but it would have been easy to discount the people she'd heard it from. Her son, however. Well, he would be hard to discount.

After a long, uncomfortable moment, Meg asked, "Wendy, what kind of medication are you taking?"

"It's called digitoxin. I have some very minor heart issues."

"That's made from foxglove," Keely said. "It speeds up the heart."

"How many pills are you missing?" I asked.

"At least twenty, maybe thirty."

"Would that be enough to kill someone?" I asked Meg.

"Yes… if you took them all at once. But that's not what we think happened, is it? We think the pills were put into the green blend so each drink would have had a much smaller dosage."

"Finn had three of the drinks. And Kathleen only had one," Louis said.

"That could explain why Kathleen's getting better," I said.

"But not why Finn is dead," Meg said. "You're assuming three drinks would be fatal. That might not be true."

"I'm getting better because I prayed to God—" Kathleen started, but her son shot her a look.

"So what if Finn was high *and* poisoned," I asked. "Do you think *that* would have killed him?"

Meg thought about it for a moment. "Digitoxin affects your heart rate. Most recreational drugs affect your heart rate. It could have been enough to kill him, yes."

Kathleen said. "None of that matters. We know who was trying to kill us and we know why."

"Does anyone have a sedative?" Heston asked.

"Heston—"

"I might have one," Wendy said. "Now, where is my bag…"

Amber stormed onto the stage. "Sorry to interrupt whatever it is you're doing, but this is very important. I'd like everyone to sign an NDA." As she said it, she held up a short stack of papers. "I've filled out your names and the date, so all you have to do is put your signature at the bottom of the page."

"Wait, you just happen to have thirteen NDAs?" I asked.

"You know Finn's reputation; I would never go anywhere

with less than twenty-five." To Louis she said, "Could I get a corner of the table? Why don't I pull yours out. You can sign it first and then maybe make me a cheese omelet."

"You can have a corner, and I'll make you an omelet, but I'm not signing anything."

"He poisoned Finn!" Kathleen said.

"No, he didn't," Heston said.

Amber looked around, uncertain. She zeroed in on the table. Louis said, "The eggs are in their shells." Then he took a piece of cheese out of one of the bowls and ate it.

"Okay, fine, make me an omelet. But do consider signing the NDA."

"I'm not signing it either, Amber," Marc said.

"Oh. Don't be like that—"

"Amber, I think there's something you need to explain," I started.

She stopped me with, "Yes, yes, I know. You *will* be paid for signing the NDA. You'll *all* be paid. The amount is filled in. You each get the same so it's fair. I thought five thousand dollars each would be appreciated."

She put the NDAs on the table with a pen. Meanwhile, Louis was melting butter for her omelet. Though he had to be at least tempted to sign, that would be ten thousand dollars for him and Marc. Ten thousand more dollars toward their house.

I asked, "Amber, why was there a syringe in your purse?"

Not expecting that question, she gasped. "It was you? *You* stole the syringe? Give it back!"

"You gave Finn drugs."

"I did not."

"Then what was the syringe for?"

She looked around the stage. Everyone had heard what we were saying and were now very interested. Finally, she said, "Adrenaline. It reverses a heroin overdose."

"So, he did take heroin," Donald said.

"He must have," Amber said. "I'm sure he must have."

"I can't say I'm surprised," Donald said. "Once a druggie always a druggie."

Except... Well, it didn't seem likely to me that Finn had shot up, gotten poisoned, *and* then been given adrenaline. Two of those maybe; three was doubtful. Two things we knew for certain were that he was poisoned like Kathleen, and that Amber, thinking he was high, gave him a shot of adrenaline. That was probably all that happened. Meaning, he was never high at all.

"Why were his pants off?"

"The adrenaline needs to be given in a thigh muscle. It's hard to do through a pair of jeans."

"Did you look for, um, tracks... before or even after he died?"

"No. But I did check the room for gear."

"And you didn't find any?"

"That doesn't mean anything, though," she said. "He's an addict. They're good at hiding things."

"He and Kathleen had the same symptoms. Symptoms that look like an overdose. You gave him adrenaline after he was poisoned." I looked at Meg. "Do you think the adrenaline is what killed him?"

She nodded her head. "Digitoxin and adrenaline could have that effect. Together they would have increased his heart rate to the point... Obviously I'm not a doctor, but I'd say it's very possible."

"Digi-what?" Amber asked. "What are you talking about?"

We explained about Wendy's pills. As we did, Amber got increasingly uncomfortable. Well, we were explaining to her that she'd killed her golden goose.

"No, someone must have given him heroin. I don't know who or how or when, but they *must* have. I couldn't have... I didn't... What you're saying is wrong. Just wrong." Gathering herself, she said, "You all need to sign an NDA. And *you* need to give me that syringe."

"No," I said.

She looked at us all, uttered a scream of frustration, then ran back toward Finn's dressing room. Meanwhile, Louis had finished her omelet and was now awkwardly holding it. After a long moment, Heston said, "If she's not going to eat that…"

"Oh no, no you don't. Heston you're not to eat anything that man makes." Then to Louis she said, "You will not poison my child."

"Are you sure you want this one?" Louis said to Heston. "I could make you one however you want it."

"Naw, it's okay." He defiantly took the omelet and went to sit next to his mother. She looked at it and her hand flew to her mouth. Clearly, she was about to be sick again. Struggling to her feet, she ran back toward the dressing rooms.

Eldridge said to me, "That thing about adrenaline reversing a heroin overdose. I think that's an urban myth."

"Really? How do you know that?"

"I'm a college student. All we talk about are class schedules and urban myths."

I felt like he was pulling my leg. And then he winked at me to confirm it.

Donald stepped in front of the *Guessmate?* desk and raised his voice to address us. "You know, since most of you are here, I want to thank you all for what you've done tonight. I know it's been challenging and, of course, terribly sad. But I know we can get through it. Now, you may have doubts about whether there will even be a reunion show after what's happened, but I can assure you that OTN is one hundred percent committed. As many of you know… I can't keep my big mouth shut, can I? …there will be a new version of *Kapowie!* reaching the airwaves soon. Which makes this reunion show very, very important. And while we're on the subject, I want you all to give a big round of applause to the star of the new *Kapowie!* Heston True."

No one applauded, but we did turn to stare at him. He had a mouthful of food, which he forced down his throat before he said, "Oh no, no, no, no, no…" He set his breakfast plate onto the floor, then stood up screaming toward the dressing rooms loud enough that she must have heard, "Kathleen! I'm going to kill you!"

Which perhaps was not the best choice of words, given the circumstances. The teenager ran toward the dressing rooms.

"Well," Donald said, looking a bit worried. "I'm sure they'll work that out. In the meantime, I think what I'd like to do with the remaining time, is record some remembrances of Finn. Positive, fond thoughts of him. Let's turn this into a memorial show. Now, I've been thinking about the order, and I'll be calling you up one by one. So be thinking of something you'd like to say about Finn on camera. Now, it is probably best that we don't directly mention his accidental death..."

"But it wasn't accidental," I said.

"You just got Amber to admit giving him the adrenaline which killed him. That was an accident."

"Someone else deliberately poisoned him. That wasn't accidental. It's at least attempted murder."

"Is it though? It could just have been a practical joke. If I remember correctly, quite a few of you enjoyed a practical joke now and then."

"Someone stole your wife's pills and put them into the drink mix, and you think that was a practical joke?"

"I wouldn't say it was in good taste... But none of that's important now. The important thing is that we go back to taping. And no one mentions things like poison and attempted murder. Let's keep that part vague."

"Keely, why don't you go first. And if you could manage a tear or two that would be terrific."

"Fuck you, Donald."

"Okay... understood. Meg, would you like to..."

"No."

"Well, where's Ricky? I know he'll do it." Then he began yelling for Ricky.

"Oh, for God's sake, Donald. Give it up," Wendy said. "It's over. We're not finishing tonight. We're going to have to go to the network, explain what happened, and sell them on the idea of a memorial show. *If* they go for it, we'll all come back another time."

"I'm not doing that for scale plus ten," Marc said.

"We'll negotiate that later," Wendy said.

"We will not," Donald said. "They'll do it for scale plus ten and be happy about it. I mean, for God's sake Wendy, coming back again doubles the budget. They'd already be making twice as much."

"For twice as much work."

"Donald, remember, we won't have to pay Finn." Wendy said. "The money's there."

Then Ricky was standing there. I had no idea how long he'd been there. Donald saw him, and said, "Ricky, we're thinking about recording some thoughts and memories about Finn. What do you say? Are you up for that?"

"There's something you should know about Finn," Ricky said. "Something I should have said earlier..."

We all looked at him, waiting.

"He killed Wes Lange."

NINETEEN

Everyone looked completely shocked. Especially Donald for some reason. Well, maybe not for *some* reason. No one was going to want a memorial episode for Finn Henderson if he was a murderer. The best Donald could hope for was an episode of *America's Most Wanted*.

And, yes, it did seem like information Rick should have mentioned earlier. It might not have anything to do with Finn's being poisoned, but it could.

"How do you know something like that?" I asked.

"I ran into him at a bar in Hollywood, early eighties. He was just blotto. He told me around the time of the wrap party for season two that he took care of Wes. They were both up for that TV show, *Young Leonardo*. It looked like Wes would be the one who got it, everyone said so. I think it was in one of those, like, gossip columns. But then Finn got it. And no one ever heard from Wes again."

"Did you think about calling the police?" Marc wanted to know.

"Are you kidding? Knowing something like that was gold. Finn paid to keep me quiet. How do you think I got all those gyms?"

"Um... from your sex tape?"

"Naw, my ex-girlfriend took three quarters of that money. I barely got enough for my condo in Studio City."

"So, you blackmailed Finn?" I pointed out.

"I wouldn't call it blackmail. He made investments in my business. That I never paid back."

"And that's all you know, Finn said he 'took care of' Wes. You don't have any details?"

"I know they went down to Compton to buy drugs for the party. While they were there, Finn paid to have him whacked. Some gang person did it. You know, some José or Jesus."

"Where's his body? Why wasn't it ever found?" Louis asked.

"My guess is he's buried under the blimp."

"What?"

"Yeah, the Goodyear blimp. They bought drugs near the place where it's kept. You know, they need this big field for landings and stuff. I think they buried him in that field."

"But you don't *know* that."

"No. But Finn would get kinda weird if you brought up the blimp."

Actually, I think I'd get weird if you casually brought up the Goodyear blimp. I mean, it's not a usual thing to work into a conversation.

"So, in all those years you never asked him any more questions about Wes?"

"Well... it's not like I saw him a lot. Once he started making movies I knew he'd have money. I went around and pitched him on the gym idea. He wrote me a check."

I looked around the stage. Everyone was paying close attention. Meg in particular looked very sad.

"This is terrible. Wes was the only one of you who was truly kind to me. The rest of you did your best to keep your distance. Especially Finn and Kathleen. They didn't want anything to do with 'the fat girl'."

"We had no idea about any of this," Wendy said. "I wish you kids had come to us with your problems. We could have helped."

"Wendy, we don't know that what he's saying is true," Donald said.

"I'm not lying," Ricky said.

"That's not what I meant. Finn told you something that might or might not be like it sounded. And my guess is it wasn't true."

"Then why did he pay me?"

"Because it was close enough to the truth that he didn't want anyone talking about it," Donald said.

"Do you know something?" I asked.

"No. But I do know the people involved. Finn could be terrible, I know that, but I don't think he'd have someone killed."

Actually, Finn's terribleness *did* seem to make him the kind of person who might have someone killed. He wasn't quite terrible enough to have done it himself. There was a real difference between hiring a murderer and being a murderer. At least in the mind of the person doing the hiring.

That's when Marc said, "Have you seen Grace recently?"

"No," I said. "Weren't you the last one with her?"

"I guess. She kicked me out of the ladies' room. Said she had to pee. But that was ages ago."

"Do you think she's still in the restroom?"

"Maybe."

"Was she okay after... the things she told us?"

"She was definitely emotional. But I'm sure... Wait, you don't think?"

"I don't know... I don't know her or what she might do."

"Did she seem distressed?" Eldridge asked.

"Yes."

"Unable to cope with her emotions?"

"Yes."

"Hopeless?"

"Oh God..."

Marc and I ran off the stage area toward the corner of the building where the restrooms were. A few moments later, we burst into the ladies' room. Grace stood next to the sink smoking a cigarette. That seemed to be what she'd been doing the whole time, since the tiny room was thick with cigarette smoke.

"My God, your faces," she said. "Did someone else—"

"You're okay! That's great!" Marc said as he rushed toward her.

"Of course, I'm okay. Why wouldn't I be... No! You didn't think I was suicidal, did you? How ridiculous. I have absolutely no intention of killing myself." She waved away some of the smoke. "At least not quickly."

"I need a cigarette," Marc said.

"I think you just need to take a few deep breaths," I pointed out.

"What's going on out there? I couldn't bear to face Donald and Wendy. Are they making people dance on Finn's grave?"

"Ricky thinks Finn had Wes killed."

She thought about that for a long moment, inhaling deeply from her cigarette. Marc went ahead and lit one of his own—though, and I'm serious, with the room flooded with smoke there hardly seemed a point.

"I suppose that would explain why Wes disappeared and no one ever heard from him again."

"Do you think someone might have known about the murder and poisoned Finn because of it?"

"Honestly, it's hard to think of anyone who'd care that much. I mean, Wes was nice to me. I think he was nice to all the girls. But he was always kind of... separate. He was a little older than we were. And I think he had a girlfriend somewhere, though she was never around. So if Ricky said Finn hired someone..."

"Yeah. The night of the wrap party."

"I wasn't there. I was starting to show, so I didn't go. I was afraid I'd be found out."

"And you never heard what happened to him?" I asked.

"I kind of remember Donald saying he went into the army. But then, honestly, I don't know when he'd have said that to me. I didn't really see anyone after the show ended. Well, Finn and Kathleen, obviously. Is there still coffee? I could really use some."

The three of us went back to the stage. Louis was at the table. Donald, Wendy and Ed were all near the camera. Ricky was on the stool so, apparently, they were attempting to film something.

"It's over, Donald," I heard Wendy saying.

"You've been trying to sabotage this show from the beginning."

"We've killed a major motion picture star. I doubt they're going to broadcast any of this."

"*We* didn't kill anyone. Your juice killed him."

"That's not true! Take it back! Take it back now!"

Okay, they were a mess. I looked around for Eldridge. He was sitting about six or seven rows up in the bleachers. I climbed up there and sat down next to him.

"Is Grace okay?"

"Yeah, I think we got a little carried away."

"It seems like that kind of night." Then he asked, "When was the last time you stayed up all night?"

The last time I'd stayed up all night was when Jeffer died. Of course I didn't want to tell him that, because... well, because I didn't really like to talk about Jeffer. But then I went ahead and told him anyway.

"The last time I stayed up all night was the night my partner, my ex—we were sort of, kinda, broken up... Anyway, he died. And I was there. At the hospital. With his family. He'd been asking for me. I'm not sure they would have called me if he hadn't been. By the time I got there he was unconscious, not speaking, not looking around. I sat with him. Told him I forgave him—which to be honest, I'm not sure I had. Actually, I'm still not sure I've forgiven him. It did seem the right thing to say at the time, though."

Eldridge didn't say anything. He just nodded and slipped his arm around me.

"Anyway, after he died that night, around two in the morning, I knew I couldn't sleep. I left the hospital. There was a time when I'd been close to his family, but when he died, well... I think I found a Denny's that was open somewhere. I ordered a breakfast but only ate a little bit of it. After that, I drove up to the Observatory, sat on the hood of my car, and watched the sun come up."

"How old was he?"

"Thirty-eight."

"AIDS?"

"Yeah." I took a deep breath and plunged onward. "Look, it's not that I don't like you. And it's not *just* that I'm your boss. It's also that I'm HIV positive. Okay? I'm guessing you're not. I mean, I hope you're not. You're so young and that would be..."

"I'm not HIV positive."

"Okay. There you go. We can't go out."

"Except we can."

"You don't want to get involved with me. I mean, I'm on these new meds and maybe they'll work, maybe they won't. There's no guarantee I'll be here in ten years."

"There's no guarantee I'll be here in ten years."

"Yeah, but—"

Was he making sense? I really wanted him *not* to make sense. But then I thought maybe it didn't have to be logical. It didn't matter whether I was scared for him or scared for me. All that really mattered was that I was too scared to go out with him.

"Did you get the virus from your partner?" he asked.

"Yes."

"It must have been so different before we knew what was happening."

"He knew what was happening."

"Oh."

"Dating me would be dangerous."

"You might not realize this, but I've never *not* had safe sex. It's smart to just assume everyone you sleep with is HIV positive. With you I wouldn't have to assume. I'd know. Seems easier, doesn't it?"

I raised an eyebrow at him. "Not what I meant. Since Jeffer died, my dating life hasn't been what you'd call… good. I went out with this one guy who ended up murdered and his body thrown into the dumpster behind Pinx. And then I dated this other guy who was murdered, stabbed right next to me in bed. That was… unpleasant. And then there's this cop—"

"I get the picture."

Well, there. That was that. He wouldn't be asking me out again. There wouldn't be any more puppy dog eyes or subtle— well, not so subtle, innuendo. Eldridge would just be my employee and anything I was feeling or trying not to feel would fade away. He'd find a boyfriend. I'd be me. And it would all be okay.

"I'm exhausted," he said. "Can I just put my head on your shoulder and close my eyes?"

"Um… okay."

He had to scrunch down a little, but he managed. It felt a little weird. I mean, I'd just told him that a typical date with me ended in death. Running for the hills screaming would have been a much more reasonable response.

We stayed like that for a few minutes. Then Louis trudged up the risers, and said, "It's after six. We should pack up. Noah, why don't you do a final round of coffee?"

TWENTY

It was nearly over. Thank God. I still had no idea who had poisoned Finn and Kathleen, but in less than sixty minutes that would be someone else's problem. I mean, not that it was ever really my problem—other than avoiding being poisoned myself and making sure Louis didn't get blamed for it.

While Eldridge and Louis began packing up, I went to the craft room and filled the coffee pot from the urn. I put sugar packets and creamers into my pockets, and grabbed a stack of Styrofoam cups. As I was about to leave, Louis popped in with a full tub.

I took the chance to ask, "Louis, did you notice anything weird about the green goop?"

"Other than the fact that it's green goop?"

"Yes, Louis, other than that."

"No. It looked like what it's supposed to be. You know, diced up mushy greens. Why?"

"I don't know. There's just... something. Something nagging at me. Probably nothing."

"Part of the point of poisoning is to make sure it goes unnoticed."

"Yeah. I'm probably just tired."

"Aren't we all."

I left the craft room and walked past the Durante room; the one Ricky had been using. He wasn't in there, but it was a mess. There were several shirts laid out over the chairs, moisturizers, bronzers and concealer on the makeup table, and an open gym bag on the floor. So I had to look inside, right? It was practically screaming at me.

The bag was almost empty. There was a pair of men's briefs —extremely brief. So brief I wondered how they held his impressive... Yes, I've seen the video. Anyway. They must be a backup pair, though why he thought he might need extra underwear... Then I noticed a folded piece of paper. I picked up the paper and unfolded it. It was an email from Wendy. The one with the list of who was having which drink.

Email was not a forte of mine. Sure, we had a Prodigy account, but Mikey took care of that. He promised me it would be useful someday, though I didn't really believe him. All of which meant it took me a moment to understand what I was looking at. The 'To:' line at the top of the page said 'rbellows19@compuserve.com'. That must be Ricky's email address. The 'From:' line said 'juicygirl22@aol.com'. That had to be Wendy. This was the email Louis told me about. In the 'cc:' line there was a string of email addresses, most of which looked like gobbledygook to me. But it could tell me who got the list even though I'd have to spend some time puzzling out whose address was whose. In the message field was a list of the cast and which drinks they'd be having.

Quickly scanning the list, I saw that all of the drinks were the ones Louis had been asked to make for the cast. Except that Kathleen was originally supposed to have a Green Goddess. Wendy had tried to change her drink, but Kathleen herself had changed it back. If one of the email addresses was Kathleen's, she'd come expecting a Green Goddess. Wendy tried to substitute a Blue Moon. Why? Was Wendy behind the poisoning? Or had she just figured out what was happening before the rest of us? But if she had figured it out, why did she let Kathleen switch?

I folded up the email and put it into my pocket, then left the dressing room. I knocked on the Zola Emory dressing room's door, but didn't wait for an answer. I just walked in.

What I found inside was frightening. Amber sat with the dead man. She was chatting with him again, this time in a much friendlier manner. Giggling as though he'd just said something funny, she stopped and looked up at me. Her eyes seemed to register just beyond sanity. Now, I know various religions and cultures have traditions of sitting with corpses, sometimes even for long periods of time, supposedly granting them peace of mind. But looking at Amber I'd have to argue against that explanation. I can't say it looked like it was bringing her much peace.

My mother had chosen a closed casket for my father's funeral. Not because he looked bad, but as my mother said, "It's bad enough he's dead. I don't want to rub people's noses in it." And Jeffer—well, in the few days between his death and his funeral, his family had turned completely against me and I was barred from attending. I have no idea if his casket was opened or closed. I'd have voted for closed.

"Should you be sitting in here?" I asked, in as kind a voice as I could muster. "You don't look well."

She just sat there, mumbling to Finn. His skin had taken on a very unnatural tone and looked remarkably waxy. I wasn't sure if he had a figure in Madame Tussauds Museum, but if he did, whatever resemblance was there before would now be more pronounced.

"Would you like a cup of coffee?" I asked because, after all, that *was* why I was there.

"When are you going to sign an NDA for me?"

"I'm not."

"Then get out."

I stepped out into the hallway and shut the door behind me. I have to say Amber wasn't doing well. Accidentally killing a movie star was apparently bad for one's health. Passing the office, I walked back out to the stage. Marc was sitting in the risers with Grace, Keely and Meg.

"Do you remember that grip from the show?" Keely was saying. "One of the union guys… Oh gosh, what was his name?"

"His name was Teddy," Meg said.

"Yes! It was. He was fine like wine."

"Do you know what happened to him?" Marc asked.

"Don't you remember? Donald fired him halfway through the second season. Well, he tried to. The union wouldn't let him, so he got paid for the rest of the season even though he didn't come to the set anymore."

"Would any of you like one last hit of coffee?" I asked.

Meg raised her cup. I filled it.

"I'm fine, thank you," Keely said. "I don't want it to keep me awake. I can't wait to get into bed."

I was about to walk away when I thought to ask, "Marc, what about the guard? When his name came up about the stunts you said, 'don't ask.' What are we not supposed to ask?"

"I meant, don't ask about the stunts. They were really lame. We'd ride a bike and do wheelies. That kind of 'stunt.' Mostly Alan was on set because his mother was Wendy's best friend."

"Oh God, yes," Keely said. "Alan… He was *not* fine like wine. Actually, he was always really creepy. I didn't even recognize him."

"Me either," Meg said.

"So… he knows Donald and Wendy pretty well?" I said.

"Yeah, he probably does." Marc looked at me suspiciously. "You think he has something to do with all this?"

"We know he jammed the doors," I said. "He could easily have also cut the phone line and disabled the fire alarm before we got here."

"But why?" Meg asked. "Why would he poison Finn and Kathleen?"

"Did they have any bad blood during the show?" I asked.

"Not that I remember."

Marc said, "Plus, it was fifteen years ago. It would have to be pretty bad blood for him to still be mad about it."

"Why do you think he's not working at a Juicy Juice?" I wondered.

"What do you mean?"

"Well, they gave him a job on the show fifteen years ago. Wouldn't working at a Juicy Juice like Ed, wouldn't that be a better job than security guard?"

"If he wanted to work at a Juicy Juice and they said no he'd have a motive," Keely said.

"To poison *them*," Marc pointed out. "Not Finn and Kathleen."

"But if it was actually Amber's shot that killed Finn..." I suggested. "Maybe the point was just to make them sick and ruin the shoot, causing some bad publicity for Juicy Juice."

"Wow, weird thought," Meg said. "If that is what's going on, then Alan has no idea Finn is dead. He's just sitting out there waiting for morning."

"Of course, that's the problem with this theory," I said. "Alan is cut off from us. If he was only trying to make Finn sick, wouldn't he want an ambulance and paparazzi here to make sure it all got in the newspaper? What would be the point of keeping us locked in all night?"

"You'd think if it was him," Meg said, "he'd have come to check on us?"

"I know, right? He'd have probably checked on us at least every two hours. He hasn't checked on us at all. It's possible Donald was telling the truth when he said Alan was afraid of losing his job if the other guard found out."

Then Donald was behind me saying, "Are you pouring coffee or are you just gossiping?"

"Oh, sorry," I said, turning to see if he had a cup. He didn't. I offered him one, which he took, and then I poured him coffee. "Do you like cream or sugar?"

"Both please."

I put the cups in the crook of my arm and pulled sugar packets and creamers out of my pocket. He had his Juicy Juice in his free hand, which he held out to me. "Can you get rid of this?"

I was already doing a juggling act.

"If you'll set it down, I'll get rid of it in a minute." I was tempted to add that I was not an octopus.

"I can't begin to tell you how tired I am of fruit smoothies," he said in a way that was meant to be friendly but failed. "Having them every day ruins them for you."

"I bet," I said, because I think he expected something like that.

Then he said, "Thank you for everything you've done, Niles." After patting my upper arm, he walked away. I glanced over at Eldridge and pulled a face. Really? Niles? Then, unfortunately, I had to follow Donald.

I asked Wendy, "Would you like a coffee?"

"No, thank you."

I raised my eyebrows in a question to Ed.

"Yeah, I'll have a cup," he said.

I poured the coffee and asked, "Cream and sugar?"

Thankfully, he took his coffee black.

I noticed Louis at the craft table. He was holding out a Juicy Juice for Eldridge. There was another in his hand. When I got there, he offered it to me and said, "I made you a smoothie."

"Yeah, I'm not sure I want that." For one, they were disgusting. For two, there was the whole issue of poisoning—though reasonably I didn't think that was a possibility. But why be reasonable?

"Don't worry, it's not one of their recipes."

"Oh."

I set the coffee pot and cups down on the table and took the drink. Eldridge was drinking his. If they were poisoned, I couldn't let him be poisoned alone, could I? From the first sip it was delicious. Chocolaty and fruity at the same time.

"What did you put in here?"

"Chocolate covered strawberries, raspberries, coconut milk, half a banana, M&Ms. Absolutely no secret anything."

"It's really good." I took a good long sip, then asked, "Are you ready to finish packing up?"

"You know, I just realized that's probably not a good idea."

"It's not a good idea to pack up? We're leaving soon."

"We're probably not leaving, though."

"What do you mean?"

Not leaving? That was a terrible thought. I was looking forward to getting into my bed. Did he think we weren't being allowed out of here?

"We're going to call the police and then we'll be here for hours being interviewed. And we shouldn't pack up because all this is evidence."

"Oh crap, it is, isn't it." Then I asked, "Do you think there might be fingerprints somewhere belonging to the someone who shouldn't have left fingerprints?"

"It's possible."

"We probably shouldn't have touched anything," Eldridge said.

"Yeah, that's what I'm realizing," Louis said. "Well, too late now."

"Then what *should* we do?" I asked.

"We have less than an hour to solve this," he said ominously.

"Oh, I don't... Can't we leave it to the police? Just this once," I begged.

"We could, but where's the fun in that?"

"I really have no idea who might have poisoned the green goop."

"Could everyone come on to the stage," Louis called out.

"Everyone." I nearly choked on my smoothie when he added, "Noah has a few questions, and then he's going to tell us all who poisoned Finn and Kathleen."

"What?! I don't know who did it!"

"I think you do."

TWENTY-ONE

My first inclination was to scream. Why was Louis doing this to me? It had been a horrible night and public humiliation wasn't going to make it any better. As people came into the stage area and spread out, I realized the only way to get through this would be to actually solve the poisonings. But how was I going to do that?

Ed leaned uncomfortably on the *Guessmate?* desk, while Donald and Wendy sat in the chairs behind it. Marc was with Grace, Keely and Meg in the front row of the risers. Eldridge and Louis stayed close to the craft table, while Ricky and Amber floated around trying to avoid each other. Kathleen and Heston came out of their dressing room and took a spot at the far end. He'd brought out a chair for his mother to sit on. In one hand she held a can of 7-Up that she occasionally sipped, and in her lap was a waste basket in case she needed to vomit again. Lovely thought.

Setting my smoothie down, I took a spot between the risers and the front of the *Guessmate?* set. As I did, I realized I was at the very end of a 1970s murder mystery. Louis had just cast me as the brilliant inspector. I might never forgive him.

In a shaky voice, I said, "All right. We're going to take this very slowly." Mainly because I had no idea what I was going to say.

"I'm sorry, what's happening?" Donald asked. "Why is Niles talking?"

"*Noah* is going to tell us who poisoned Finn and Kathleen," Louis said. "He's really very good at this."

"This isn't a party game, someone died," Wendy said.

"I'm not going to sit here—" Donald said.

"Where else are you going to be? Are you going to leave? We'd all like to leave," Louis said. "And we could if you hadn't had the guard jam the doors!"

"Donald, maybe you should just shut up for once," Wendy said. Then she looked at me and said dryly, without confidence, "All right, go ahead. Tell us who killed Finn."

"Okay. I will," I swallowed hard before I began. "First, let's think about motive. Four of us didn't know the victims until tonight. Me, Louis, Eldridge and Ed."

"You could be deranged fans," Donald said.

"True. But how would we have even known about the taping? It wasn't publicized anywhere."

"But..."

"And how would we, as deranged fans, get ourselves invited in the first place?"

"Well..."

"As I was saying, four of us have no motive. Now, let's look at the cast. The person with the strongest motive in the cast is probably Kathleen."

"What? That's ridiculous. What are you talking about?" She said, her voice quivering.

"You had a motive, Kathleen, your son—"

And then I stopped. *Oh God. Did I want to be the one to tell Heston his dad had died a few hours ago?* The silence hung over me like a pendulum out of a Vincent Price movie. Then, Heston said, "It's okay. I know Finn was my birth father. And I know Grace is my real mom."

"Oh!" Grace peeped. "You know? I had no idea…"

"I found the adoption papers in Kathleen's desk a while back. I'm not very well supervised."

"That is *not* true," Kathleen said. "Heston is loved and well taken care of. We almost always know where he is. And what you're saying is absurd. I have no motive whatsoever."

"Keeping Heston from finding out who his birth parents are would be a motive."

"Yes, but he already knew."

"But you didn't know he knew. You're just finding that out now."

"You're forgetting *I* was poisoned too!"

"You could have poisoned yourself just enough to make you sick to keep anyone from suspecting you."

"Suspecting me? *Me?* But I am a good Christ—"

"Yeah. Whatever. The bigger problem with this theory is that you went into your dressing room as soon as we got here and, as nearly as I can tell, you didn't come out until after Finn had drunk his first Juicy Juice. Did anyone see her come out?"

They all just looked at me. No one had.

"Heston?"

"We were in there the whole time." He sounded a little disappointed, as though he'd have been happy his mother was the poisoner.

"So she couldn't have put the poison into the drink mix. Neither of you could."

"Unless they're both lying," Donald said.

"Did anyone see them out of their dressing room during that time?"

No one said anything. I moved on.

"Grace had a motive. Finn got you pregnant and then Kathleen practically bought your child."

"How dare you—"

Kathleen's outrage was getting tiresome.

"I would never have gone that far…" Grace said. "It's unfair."

"She was with me, though," Marc said. "In the dressing room. She couldn't have poisoned the drinks either."

"And we were together, too," Keely said. "Neither Meg or I could have done it."

"You're right. Though you both had motives."

"Not strong motives," Meg said. "Not ones that would fester for fifteen years."

"I'll concede that. And then there's Ricky," I said. "You were blackmailing Finn. Had he decided not to pay you anymore?"

"Hold on," he said. Pointing at Meg and Keely he said, "Those two know about poison plants. And we all got an email about who was having which drink. They could have mushed up some poison plants beforehand to bring with them."

"But no one saw them near the craft room."

"No... But if they were in it together—"

"You seem very interested in deflecting the blame."

"I'm just pointing out you might not be as smart as you think you are," he said.

And he was probably right there. I probably wasn't as smart as I thought I was. But I had no choice but to continue.

"You can relax. I don't think you did it. Even if you only intended to make Finn sick as a threat, I don't think you'd have taken the chance of killing your golden goose. Sure, now you're attempting to blackmail his estate, but how long will that last? Once the secrets are out there you have no leverage."

He got an unhappy look on his face that told me he hadn't thought it all the way through. He hadn't realized his gravy train was going to end.

I paused. I was almost through everyone in the room and I still hadn't identified a killer. "That brings us to Amber. You did *actually* kill Finn."

"That was a mistake. I thought he'd taken heroin. I didn't do anything wrong. I was trying to save him!"

"Yeah... I think it's still considered negligent homicide."

"Homicide? No, no, no. A mistake... I had good intentions."

"Okay. Maybe they'll go with involuntary manslaughter. Provided they can't also connect you to the poison."

"What? No..."

"You seem prepared to make the most of Finn's death. In fact, too prepared."

"He was a drug addict. Of course I thought about what might come afterward. Of course I was prepared for that. And you're wrong. Nothing's going to happen to me. I made a mistake. I thought he'd taken an overdose. I was trying to *save* him."

"I believe you," I said. Which didn't mean she wasn't in a lot of trouble, but it seemed best not to rub that in. Then I said, "Which brings us to Donald and Wendy."

"Neither of us have a motive," Donald said.

"You *both* have a motive. You don't want to be in the juice business and your wife doesn't want to be in show business."

"I would never—" Wendy began. Then she turned to her husband and said, "You wouldn't dare."

"Of course, I wouldn't. Don't listen to a word that this, this... person says."

"I didn't say you did it. I said, you both have a motive. The thing is, poisoning Finn and later Kathleen would not get either of you what you want."

"You've run out of people," Donald said. "Are you saying none of us did it?"

I decided to ignore that because he was right; I had run out of people. And he was wrong; I did think one of them did it.

"We know for certain Finn and Kathleen were each poisoned with a juice drink by someone in this room." I let that sink in for just a moment. "Each of them had a drink with the green mix as an ingredient. The remaining green mix has disappeared—which is how I know it has to be someone here. The green mix was made at the Juicy Juice in North Hollywood and picked up by Louis in the afternoon. There are three possibilities: It might have been poisoned at the store; while it was in Louis' possession;

or while it was in the craft room. All we know for certain is that when Finn drank it at around eleven thirty it had already been poisoned."

I took a long, dramatic pause. I didn't intend for it to be dramatic. I simply needed time to figure out what I wanted to say next.

"We also know that a large amount of Wendy's medicine has gone missing. Someone removed it from her bag and returned it to Donald's. Wendy noticed the medicine was missing around midnight."

"That's right," Wendy said.

"But if it was used as poison, then it had to be taken from your bag before eleven-thirty."

Something began to fall into place for me. Something I'd been trying to understand for a while.

"Or... *well* before eleven-thirty. Louis didn't notice anything odd about the mix. That means the pills must have been dissolved and mixed in. There had to be enough time to do that. Louis picked the cooler of fruit up yesterday afternoon. It's possible the green goo—um, the proprietary mix was already poisoned."

"That's not... No," Wendy said, "that didn't happen."

"It could have been done here in a few minutes in one of the restrooms, I suppose. And then whoever it was must have looked for a chance to slip into the craft room and mix it into the green goop. But it doesn't seem likely. Someone would have seen them. Wendy, who knows you take digitoxin?"

"My doctor, of course."

"Of the people here. Who knows?"

"You and Meg..."

"Who knew before eleven-thirty?"

"Donald, of course..."

"Okay, I thought we've already decided I'm innocent," he said impatiently.

"Well... anyone could have looked in my bag," Wendy said.

"Do you always carry the medication with you?"

"I have been. Yes. I keep forgetting to take the damn things. It's better if they're always with me. It's the only way I might remember."

"So you had your bag with you when you went to your store yesterday afternoon."

Wendy fidgeted anxiously. "Hold on. You said yourself poisoning them wouldn't get me what I wanted."

"It wouldn't have. But it would get Wes Lange what he wants."

"What?"

Actually, several people said, "What?" I'd surprised them. To be honest, I'd surprised myself.

"No..." Ricky said. "He's dead. I told you."

"You told us Finn said he 'took care of' Wes. Sending him to prison would take care of him. Fifteen years in prison is a good reason to hold a grudge."

"Wes isn't here," Donald said. "How could he kill Finn if he's not even here."

"He is here, though. He's right there." I pointed at Ed, who wasn't Ed. "One of you said there was a rumor Wes went to prison. He has a prison tattoo next to his thumb. He said he'd been learning carpentry. That's the kind of thing they teach you in prison."

"He doesn't look anything like Wes," Ricky said.

"And you don't look the way you did fifteen years ago, do you?"

Turning to Ed, I said, "You were the one who got the cooler of fruit ready, weren't you? And you knew about Wendy's medical condition. You also had the list of who was supposed to drink what so that you'd assemble enough fruit. How long have you been waiting for an opportunity like this?"

He stood there for a few moments looking like he might make a run for it... but there was nowhere to run. Very quietly, he said, "Fifteen years. Fifteen years I've been planning this. Waiting for payback."

"Weird things have been happening since we got here," I said. "Marc's cigarette case, Meg's troll doll, Grace's photograph... That was you, wasn't it?"

He nodded.

"You wrote cocksucker on my mirror?" Ricky said.

Now Ed smiled and said, "I did."

"Fuck you."

"You were outside my house filming me," Kathleen said, assuming that he was responsible for the videotape of her and Finn.

He said, "Yeah... I, uh, did that."

"You monster!"

Of course, I knew he hadn't done any such thing. I knew it was actually Heston who'd made the video. But Ed kept his mouth shut and took the blame. The boy looked sheepish. I think he knew he should tell the truth, but he also knew that his mother wasn't someone you told the truth to.

"What about me?" Keely said. "You didn't leave anything for me."

"The flowers," he said. "I'm the one who ordered the flowers. It was easy to get on Wendy's email. And I left the money in an envelope at your shop. I knew you did beautiful work."

"I knew something was funny about that. Actually getting paid, I mean. That was the tip-off. Thank you."

I suppose it was kind of him, but it was also... He'd made sure there was foxglove in the display. He must have known...

"You thought you'd get away with this," I said.

"I didn't think anyone would die."

Donald walked up close to him and looked him over. "Are you *sure* you're Wes Lange? You really don't look at all like him."

"My face is a little different. I got beat up a few times in prison."

"Oh." Donald backed up.

"Is Ed your real name?" I asked. He'd have had to give Donald and Wendy documents to get the job.

"Yeah. Ed Urbanski. When I applied for the job six months ago, I didn't think they'd remember. And they didn't. They never had much to do with the money."

"Wes, tell us what happened," Grace said. "How did you end up in prison?"

"Finn wanted some coke for the wrap party. I drove him down to Compton so he could make the deal. He went into this house, came out, and put a gym bag in my trunk. I didn't think anything about it. Then before we got to the freeway, we were pulled over. He'd put twenty kilos of cocaine into my trunk. He was doing favors for the dealers so he didn't have to pay for his coke. He'd said something about running an errand before the party. I think he was delivering the drugs for them. When I met with an attorney, he said the only way to get out of it was to turn in the people from the house, but I didn't know anything about them. Finn did. That's when I found out Finn had already made a deal. He'd told the cops I was the one with the connection. That I'd asked him to go into the house to cover my ass. That he didn't know anything, and that I was the one who knew it all. Except I didn't know anything."

Then he turned to Donald, and said, "And it was all your fault."

"Wes, we only tried to help you."

"You *helped* me into prison. For fifteen years."

"We got you an attorney."

"After you got one for Finn. You knew his attorney was going to blame everything on me. You knew the drugs weren't mine, you *knew* they were Finn's. You only got me an attorney so you wouldn't look bad."

"I was trying to protect the show. It was better—"

"The show was over."

"I didn't know that, though. Finn promised to stay with the show. He promised he'd do another season after *Young Leonardo* wrapped. That would have turned us into a huge hit. I couldn't let him go to prison for drugs."

"But I could. You didn't care that I was innocent."

Weakly, Donald said, "That's not true." It was clear that it was though.

There was no point in continuing, Donald would never admit he'd done anything wrong. I asked Ed, "Why trap us in here? Was that necessary?"

"I didn't... I didn't know that Donald was going to have the doors jammed. I thought Finn would drink the poison and we'd call an ambulance. The medicine bottle was in Donald's camera bag, I thought he'd get blamed. That's what I'd planned."

"I don't think that's true," I said. "Trapped in here, unable to communicate with the outside world. That can't be a coincidence."

"*I* cut the phone line," Amber admitted.

"You?"

"Finn was nervous about tonight. About facing Kathleen. That kind of thing is always a risk for an addict. He didn't bring his mobile phone because he was afraid of calling a dealer. That's why I had the adrenaline with me. That's why I cut the phone line right after we got here."

"And the fire alarm?"

"That was me," Ed said. "After Finn died, I panicked. I didn't know what to do. I wanted time to think." Then he added, "The key to the elephant door is on a hook next to the lever. If we'd been in danger—"

And that's when I remembered him telling us the guard had the key. Why had we trusted him? He was a complete stranger.

And then we heard the door open, and Alan called out... "Okay, time to go home."

TWENTY-TWO

"I'd still like everyone to sign an NDA," Amber said as we stepped through the door. No one paid her any attention. "No, seriously, I'd like you all to sign. Ten thousand dollars. Each. How about that? I can write the checks this afternoon…"

But by then we didn't care about money. Or more likely, didn't believe her. All we wanted was to be out in the open air. Standing right outside the soundstage the sun was already up, but it was still cool. Even though June gloom hung heavily overhead, it felt like we were basking in the light.

"You need to call the police," Louis was telling the guard.

"But, does he?" Donald asked.

"Yes, he does" Wendy said. "This is over, whether you like it or not."

"I bet you're happy about that."

"No, I'm not happy. Someone died, Donald."

"My dreams died."

"Oh my God!"

Amber interrupted, "If you're not going to sign an NDA, I'd like to talk to you about what you *are* going to say."

"Amber, we're going to tell the truth," Marc said.

"Oh, please don't do that!"

And then the police where there. First one black-and-white, then another. An ambulance showed up, followed by police detectives and eventually the coroner. Ed and Amber were taken into custody fairly quickly. Amber was crying that it wasn't her fault, that it was an accident. My bet was the prescription for the adrenaline was in her name. I was pretty sure giving someone your prescription drugs was a crime in itself. For Amber, this was only going to get worse. She definitely needed a lawyer. She could even end up in more trouble than Ed. All he had to deal with was attempted murder.

Once again adorned with her scarf and sunglasses, Kathleen threw a fit when she wasn't immediately taken to the hospital—though she'd stopped vomiting a couple of hours ago. An EMT checked her out and said she should just call her doctor and have him check her out.

"I was poisoned! On purpose! A hate crime. A hate crime against all Christians!"

Honestly, I was glad I'd never be seeing her again. Well, except for the news reports. I'd be seeing her in those a lot during the next few weeks. The police were almost immediately followed by photographers, paparazzi who would have been devastated if they missed an event like Finn Henderson's death. I wondered if Amber had tipped them off, though I hadn't seen her use her mobile. But then I wondered which of the photographers probably had police scanners? A careful purchase at Circuit City could get you all the information you needed.

When the coroner brought Finn's body out on a stretcher with a sheet over it, dozens of flash bulbs went off as the photographers grabbed shots of the gurney being put into the back of the waiting ambulance. Even after the ambulance doors were closed, the flash bulbs continued. It was only after the ambulance drove off that they stopped.

There were journalists among the photographers, and they descended on us, asking questions. They recognized Kathleen, of course, so she got the brunt. She raised a hand in the air toward

God, and in a loud, strong voice asked everyone to pray with her for Finn's eternal soul. No one seemed to join her, but the cameras went into overdrive, which had probably been the entire point.

It took a little more than two hours before the four of us had each given a statement and were allowed to go home. Before we got into the car to finally leave, Marc said goodbye to Grace and Meg and Keely. There were lots of hugs and promises to keep in touch that likely would not be followed up on.

By the time we were able to go home around ten that morning, I had a stomachache from so much coffee. Louis had made another giant pot of it once it became clear we'd all have to stay and talk to the police. He was right that they didn't want us to take anything away. In fact, it was a little surprising they allowed him to make more coffee.

The upside of all that was we didn't have to pack the car. At least not that morning. We drove to my store, which was already open by that time. Carl and Denny had come in early since I'd known I'd need to get some sleep. Of course, I'd thought I'd be at least two hours into my day's sleep by then, but that hadn't happened.

I got out of the car with Eldridge after he said goodbye to Marc and Louis. I needed a moment with him.

"Look, I doubt we're ever going to get paid for that event, so I'm just going to add what you were promised into your check."

"It's not your fault."

"I know but... well, I did get you involved so I feel at least a little—"

And then he leaned over and kissed me. He stayed there for a long moment with his lips pressed to mine. I tried to resist, I really did. But I had to kiss him back... had to. He put his arm around my waist and pulled me closer. I was pressed up against him with my hand around his neck. I knew I should be remembering to breathe, but it didn't seem to be important at the time.

Nothing seemed important except kissing him... And then he stopped.

"We'll consider that my payment."

We would not. I still planned to pay him.

"I should go," he said.

"Right. You're right. You should go. Good-bye."

I climbed back into the car as quickly as I could. As we pulled away from the curb, Louis looked over from the front seat and said, "Solved a murder *and* got kissed. I'd said you've earned a nap."

And it *was* my intention to take a nap. But when I lay down, I couldn't stop thinking about Ed. I felt bad for him. The people he'd tried to punish *did* actually deserve it. Well, not death, obviously. But that hadn't been his plan. As I thought about it, making the person who'd gotten you sent to prison for fifteen years violently ill wasn't really justice. It didn't balance the scales. Not that I could see a way to do that.

And Heston. Ed had taken the blame for the video Heston had used to expose his mother and Finn. That was kind. Though I imagine Heston must have thought his mother would eventually find out he was behind it. He must have been ready for her ire, but then Ed had let him off the hook. I would have probably let him off the hook myself. Or I hope I would have. The kid had enough problems.

After lying in bed for nearly an hour, I got up and called my mother.

"Oh my God!" she said when she answered. "Finn Henderson is dead!"

"Yes, I know. I was there."

"Did you get me an autograph?"

"You said you didn't want one."

"Well, I didn't know he was going to die."

"And neither did I."

"That poor boy."

"Yes, it is sad," I said. "And sad that we didn't take it seriously. We thought he was back on drugs."

"Well, it makes sense. He was acting like he was high."

"Okay, who did you talk to?"

"Marc. Louis. And Leon."

"Leon wasn't there."

"That doesn't mean he doesn't know everything that happened."

I had to admit that could be true. In fact, he probably knew more than I did.

"So you already know everything that happened. What are we going to talk about?"

"You can tell me about your boyfriend."

"Eldridge is *not* my boyfriend."

"And yet you knew who I was talking about."

I was very tempted to say 'Angie, back off,' just the way Heston True spoke to his mother. Instead I said, "Mom, could you maybe, I don't know, mind your own business?"

"Whether you're happy or not *is* my business."

"Oh God."

"I'm going to meet Eldridge eventually."

"Because he works for me."

"You kissed him."

"He kissed me." A very technical point, I know. And not entirely true. "I'm going to kill Marc and Louis. So there, you're responsible for a double murder. And you'll only ever see me on visiting day."

She sighed heavily. "All right. We've gone too far. I'm sorry. But it's only because we love you."

"I know. Maybe you could love me a little less."

"No. I absolutely will not. I *will* try to give you a little more space, and I'll ask Marc and Louis to do the same."

"And Leon."

"Oh sweetheart, you can't expect miracles."

And then I yawned. She must have heard because she asked, "Why aren't you sleeping?"

"I tried to, but I couldn't. Maybe I can now."

"Maybe you can. Get some rest, dear."

"Well…" Leon said. "I'm sorry someone died, but being right is one of the most delicious things in life. I'm so glad I wasn't there."

"It was a lot to happen in one night," I said.

"Don't be ridiculous. I've fallen in love three times in one night. All you had to contend with was one tiny celebrity death."

It was around seven that Sunday night. Louis had thrown together what he considered a 'simple' little dinner: spinach salad, angel hair pasta in a pesto cream sauce and pistachio ice cream. It didn't take long to figure out the theme of the evening was green.

"You're not planning to poison us, are you?" I asked with a bit more snark than usual. But then I was operating on four hours of sleep. I was hopeful the chardonnay would knock me out for at least ten.

"I have to say I feel a bit bad for Ed—I mean, Wes," Louis said. "No, I guess I mean, Ed."

"Only because you always like a bear," Marc said.

"Not just that… He wasn't trying to *kill* anyone."

"That works out better if you don't poison people," Leon said.

"Maybe they'll go easy on him," I said.

"Even if they do, I think he was on parole, which means he'll have to finish that sentence before the new sentence can even begin. The best he can hope for is involuntary manslaughter. But they'll probably try to prove attempted murder."

"If he'd only been able to let go of the past," Marc said.

"It's hard for people to let go of the past," I said, a prime example myself. There was a lot I hadn't let go of.

"I let go of the past every single day," Leon said.

I shifted in my seat, tempted to ask if he really thought that was true but terrified of the answer. I turned to Louis, and said, "I have to ask. Why did you do that to me? Why did you push me forward and make me solve everything?"

"I realized you were the only one who could. I'd been too busy making smoothies and omelets to really know what was happening. And Marc had spent most of the night gossiping with his old friends. Meanwhile, you'd been serving coffee, running errands. Watching everyone. It suddenly seemed to me the only person who would have enough information was you. And I was right, wasn't I?"

I had the feeling there was more to it than that. Still, I said, "When I started talking, I had no idea what I was going to say."

"I knew you'd find your way."

"Well, Marc" Leon said. "You haven't said whether it was nice seeing all your old friends?"

"Old, yes. Friends, I'm not so sure. A couple of them tried to pin the whole thing on Louis."

"To be fair, I *was* the one passing out poison smoothies."

Marc gave him a stern look. "You had no idea."

"Of course not. That's why I'm not in jail right now. Speaking of jail did you see O.J.'s mug shot?"

And then we talked about O.J. for quite a while. There'd been several articles on the front page of the *Los Angeles Times*, though it didn't give much new information. Which didn't prevent us from examining each and every detail.

Eventually, Leon began humming "Can You Feel the Love Tonight", before he said to me, "How is the romance going?"

Louis cleared his throat and tried to subtly shake his head. Apparently, my mother's word was her bond and she'd already had a chat with him.

Leon looked confused for a moment, then said, "It was just a question."

"Louis," Marc said. "We're going to see *The Lion King* this week. Wednesday night."

"We are? Isn't that for kids?"

"Kids and gays. I got advance tickets at the El Capitan for the ten o'clock show. It's going to be all gay men, trust me. Plus, there's a stage show."

"A stage show with lions. How could I resist?"

"You're going to love it."

"Yes, sir."

Then they talked about Disney musicals for quite some time.

It seemed awful that Ed was going back to prison. I mean, he shouldn't have done the things he did, but then the things that were done to him shouldn't have happened either. He wasn't a bad person, which in some ways made it better and in other ways made it worse.

After the ice cream, Marc said, "My mother called this afternoon."

"That was fast," I said.

"It was."

"What did you say to her?"

"I told her I'd never give them another dime. She got very insulted, told me what a horrible son I've been, and hung up. I don't expect I'll hear from them again."

"What would have been the right response?" I asked, actually curious.

He thought about it a moment before he said, "She could have said she understood why I might be suspicious and then promise to never ask me for another cent."

"You're very kind," Leon said. "I think the only correct response would have been to offer you cash. Immediately."

"That's not going to happen. But at least it's over."

I bit later I said good night. As I walked to the stairs leading up to my apartment, Louis called out, "Sweet dreams."

"Yeah. I'm going to give that a try."

The next afternoon, I went into the store. Mikey had already created a display of all the Finn Henderson videos we had to rent. Most of them had already been rented, so the display looked pathetic. We discussed ordering more, but there was a question about whether they'd arrive in time. People would be moving on to something else soon enough. For instance, O.J. Simpson looked like he'd be occupying the front page for some time.

Eldridge arrived around five. He and I would be working the evening shift alone after Mikey left. There was generally a rush from five to about seven-thirty. People stopping in after work to grab something to watch that night. It was a small rush, given that it was a Monday, but it was a rush all the same.

Around eight, after Mikey had been gone for a while and the rush was over, the store was basically empty. Eldridge and I had just finished reshelving videos, when I decided to ask, "So what are we going to do on this date?"

He tried to hide how happy he was that I'd given in, but didn't do a good job of it. "Well, I think we should have dinner. Somewhere nice but not too nice. And then we should go to a movie. And afterward we can talk about the movie for a very long time while we walk around the city."

"It's going to need to be a very interesting movie."

"It will be when we get done talking about it."

"What do you want to see?" I braced myself, expecting something in Italian or Japanese.

"*Four Weddings and a Funeral*."

"Isn't that a little on-the-nose for a first date?"

"It's about a guy who doesn't want to commit. See? There'll be lots to talk about."

"Uh, yeah… there will be."

LOUIS' LAVENDER SHORTBREAD

Ingredient list:

    4 tsp. dried lavender

    1 1/2 lbs. unsalted butter at room temperature

    3/4 cup cane sugar

    3/4 cup confectionery sugar

    1/2 cornstarch

    2 tsp. vanilla extract

    1 tsp. salt

    7 cups unbleached white flour

I recommend a very warm day for this recipe, since you'll want the butter to soften.

I grow a pot of English lavender outside my apartment door. It's getting quite large. When it blooms, I harvest the flowers, hang them in my kitchen and allow them to dry. When you're ready to cook with them, separate the flowers from the stem and chop until the flowers are very small.

Many recipes call for only cane sugar. I use a mix of sugar and confectionery sugar. It creates a smoother texture.

In order, mix the ingredients together then form into squares or fingers. You can also roll them out and make cookies if you like.

Chill before baking at 300 degrees. They should cook until the edges are just brown 12-15 minutes, depending on what shape you chose.

LOUIS' CRAFT TABLE JUICY JUICE

Ingredient list:
    Chocolate-covered strawberries
    Raspberries
    1/2 Banana
    Coconut milk
    M&Ms
    1 big scoop of frozen yogurt

Put it all into a blender. Blend for as long as it takes. Avoid all chalky protein powders.

Year of the Rat

A Mean Season

The Happy Month

IN THE WYANDOT COUNTY SERIES

The Less Than Spectacular Times of Henry Milch

A Fabulously Unfabulous Summer for Henry Milch

The Fall and Rise of Henry Milch

OTHER BOOKS

The Perils of Praline

Desert Run

Full Release

The Ghost Slept Over

My Favorite Uncle

Femme

Praline Goes to Washington

Aunt Belle's Time Travel & Collectibles

Masc

Never Rest

Code Name: Liberty

Fathers of the Bride

Sentenced to Christmas

ABOUT THE AUTHOR

Marshall Thornton writes several popular mystery series, most notably the *Boystown Mysteries* and the *Pinx Video Mysteries*. He has won the Lambda Award for Gay Mystery three times. His books *Femme* and *Code Name Liberty* were Lambda finalists for Best Gay Romance. Other books include *My Favorite Uncle, The Ghost Slept Over* and *Fathers of the Bride.* He holds an MFA in Screenwriting from UCLA.